Babette's Pack

Babette's Pack

A HEARTWARMING AND INSPIRATIONAL DOG STORY OF A SPUNKY LITTLE SHIH TZU WITH UNCANNY ABILITIES

Kathryn Walter

To order additional copies of this book, contact:
Xlibris LLC
1-888-795-4274
www.Xlibris.com
Orders@Xlibris.com
138629

Contents

I would like to dedicate this book to those people who breathe joy into my life. My dear husband Bob, and the wonderful strong women who lift me to the sun: my daughter, Megan; my sister, Debbie; and my best friend, Kathy. These people whispered success in my ears when I was doubtful, and I could not have gone forward without their love and support. Last but certainly not least, *Babette's Pack* is dedicated to dog lovers all over the world, for they are my brethren.

Chapter I

MR. WONDERFUL

Kat was an "air force brat," the name given to children of career air force officers and NCOs who followed them from station to station. With her mother, younger sister, and five younger brothers, Kat changed homes, schools, and friends every two or three years. She now found herself living in Aviano, Italy, and freshly graduated from the Vicenza American High School, a boarding school in Vicenza, Italy, devoted to air force dependents. Slender and with blue-green eyes and long, straight blonde hair and a turned-up nose, she would describe herself as a typical California girl (with perhaps a little more "junk in the trunk than she would have preferred). She was the stepdaughter of an air force pilot stationed at Aviano Air Base. As the oldest of seven children ranging in age from six months to eighteen years, she was expected to help shepherd the herd during family relocations and to help shoulder the hard work of maintaining a household of seven children when the father was routinely away for weeks at a time. She developed the level of maturity and sense of responsibility that entails. Having now graduated from high school, her parents believed her to be mature enough to date an air force man, something that had been verboten before.

Most military families stationed in a foreign land will be there for three years and then rotate to a new station. To live in a foreign country means learning a new language, a new culture, and new customs.

The language barrier alone made even the most mundane chores an adventure. Need a quick loaf of sliced bread for dinner? Run out of dog food on a Saturday night? Good luck!

Shopping for clothes entailed almost a legal battle because when shopping in an open-air Italian market, you'd better be prepared to engage in some high-level bargaining. Buying a pair of shoes was exhausting, like fighting in a war—but done good-naturedly. The Italians so loved to bargain that yelling, threatening, obscene gestures, and stomping away and returning with an entirely different offer were all anticipated and expected behaviors during a transaction. Strolling through an Italian marketplace overwhelmed one's senses with a cacophony of wheedling, pleading, and threatening that accompanied every purchase. Since many Americans find these cultural differences intimidating, armed-forces bases are provided with many of the conveniences of home, such as a grocery store (the commissary), a department store (the base exchange), a dry cleaner, a beauty shop, a snack bar, etc. That means relying upon and traveling to the base to have the conveniences of home, which makes the base a somewhat-cloistered community.

The young people in particular suffered a kind of culture shock. If the movie playing at the base theater had been seen or was ancient, often the case as American movies were hard to come by overseas, then there was little available in the way of entertainment in the immediate area. There was no McDonald's, Bob's Big Boy, or Carl's Jr. to hang out in, but there was a snack bar—the headquarters that was used to meet, grab a hamburger, or just plain hang out with friends.

So it was that Kat sat in the fluorescent-lit snack bar, smelling the hamburger grease and squinting to read the *Air Force Times*. She contemplated her mission: to meet "Mr. Wonderful." She had given the matter a lot of thought since graduating from high school two months before. She had actively "inspected the troops," looking over the local talent until she found herself thunderstruck by a certain young airman. As one of the few dateable-aged American females on a remote air-base site in Aviano, Italy, she was pretty close to guaranteed to have her pick of whatever air force men were stationed at the small air base. She had been admonished by her parents that since her father was an officer, it would only be proper to date a man on base who was also an officer. As a rule, fraternization between the enlisted ranks and officers was frowned upon. Plus, her mother reminded her for the nth time that it was just as easy to fall in love with a successful, well-educated officer as it was to fall for a poorly paid young airman. This was as much incentive to Kat as a red flag to a bull to do just the opposite.

The gentleman in question—Mr. Right, that is—was a friend of an airman buddy named Doug, who Kat had already shaken down for information. Doug said the guy's name was Bob; Bob was an air traffic controller and hailed from Pennsylvania. According to Doug, Bob was recently unattached, though he was never at a loss for female companionship even in this climate of slim pickings. He promised to introduce her. Kathryn peered from under her *Air Force Times* newspaper to secret a look at the gorgeous, dark-haired airman, who sat there quietly. She steeled herself, remembering a favorite saying that her father used when tackling a problem: "Faint heart never won fair maiden." It was the time to act; it was now or never.

She strolled across the base exchange's snack bar, tossing her long hair that was gathered in a ponytail high on the top of her head. Her jeans tight enough to see through and with a short shirt flashing glimpses of a bare midriff, she was trying her best to look nonchalant yet sexy for all her eighteen years.

As she approached the table where Bob and several friends sat, including Doug, she said "Hi" louder than she needed, hoping to get Bob to look up and notice her. But he had his head bowed, focusing intently on a crossword puzzle. This may not be as simple as she had planned.

She stole another glance at Bob. What a hunk! His gorgeous face was dominated by expressive brown eyes framed with thick curtains of long dark eyelashes, always a crowd pleaser in her book. He was clean-shaven with soft rounded features, full lips, and a heart-shaped face, and his physique—incredible. He was wafer-thin at the waist with broad shoulders, a flat stomach, and impressive biceps. Everything about him screamed strength. Not only his breath-stopping build, but he had a self-assured manner about him that was at once gentle and powerful. He was quiet not as a consequence of being shy but because he felt no need for inane chatter. Kat was a goner.

She kicked Doug's foot; he looked up and remembered their conversation. "Oh, hi, Kat," he said with a knowing look on his face. He allowed a smile to dance across his handsome features and teased her a little, stalling on the introduction he promised. Then he introduced her to the *other* two airmen at the table. "Justin, Greg, this is Kathryn, or Kat. She just graduated from high school and works for the dispensary."

Greg looked up with a come-hither smile on his face and said, "Well, sit on down here, girl. Can I get you something to drink?"

She replied, "That would be great."

Kat sat in the only available chair, which was not nearly close enough to Bob, and suffered through the introductions, barely responding or even breathing. Greg returned with a Coke. She thanked him and sipped on the straw. Finally, Doug let her off the hook. "Hey, Bob, this is Kat. Her dad is a pilot. Bob is an air traffic controller and may even have talked to your dad from the tower."

Bob looked up with very little interest and made polite conversation.

Kat was so nervous that for all practical purposes, she was dumbstruck even after all the work she had gone through to get the introduction. First, she stuttered when she told him how long she had lived in Italy. Stuttered! Then she forgot the name of the doctor she worked for at the dispensary. If that wasn't humiliating enough, she spilled her Coke, managing to get plenty on Bob's freshly starched fatigues.

Kat excused herself and stumbled away from the table in disgust as the Rolling Stones blared from the jukebox; "(I Can't Get No) Satisfaction" rang in her ears. She was angry at herself because she had clearly not made the impression on Bob she had hoped to make but was *determined* to try again. "Oh yeah," she mumbled to herself. "It's on."

Bob never had a chance. Kat pestered Doug to fix them up until she finally wrangled a double date with him, his girl, Bob, and herself. They went to a mediocre show at the base theater and then went out to eat. Ordering in broken Italian with gestures resembling sign language, they got the world's best pizza, uniquely Italian, with anchovies and artichoke hearts.

From that day forward, Bob and she were joined at the hip. Anyone who does not believe that opposites attract has never witnessed the kind of chemistry that can take place between a sternly reared Pennsylvanian Mennonite man and a born and bred California girl. Every quality not so well developed in Kat, Bob brought to the table; every quality not so well developed in Bob, Kat contributed. Their qualities combined, making each a better person together than either separately. Her gregariousness and love of fun was tempered by his quiet intelligence and reserved demeanor. To her, he was "Bobby." His sometimes-imposing countenance that earned him a reputation for being a bit distant was suspended for the girl. He could be affectionate and funny with a seldom-seen dry sense of humor. When she looked at him, he saw his greatness reflected in her eyes and pledged right then and there to be that person she saw. She saw him as the kind of man she could respect and with whom she could build a meaningful life.

The two had all the considerable wonder and romance of Italy at their feet. They made fast friends with the Guido and Lorena, young Italians living in the area, playing baseball and drinking wine together on the weekends. Their new friends spoke English but insisted Kat and Bob speak only Italian, forcing them to improve their Italian-language skills.

They often caught the train to Mestre and then took a ferry to Venice, where they did their best and most memorable dating. Venice is enchanting with the storybook canals, gondolas, and the Bridge of Sighs, which is what the tourists know of Venice. But Kat and Bob knew the spots the locals frequented where a tourist was never spotted. They danced till the wee hours at a nightclub called El Souk, or they gorged on stuffed pizza soufflé at Ristorante Pizziaoli across La Scala Opera house. Sometimes they just sat, talked, and drank strong espresso with lemon peel in the Piazza San Marco while watching the pigeons playing the clown for bits of bread. Venice was their stomping ground.

Aviano was a sleepy little town, located at the foot of the Dolomites, with narrow streets and picturesque hotels. Every day after a monster lunch, the entire city closed down for a siesta. Nothing got done between 1:00 PM and 3:00 PM. The Italians are a warm, affectionate people with a clear idea of the finer things in life, like good wine, exquisite pasta, and long afternoon naps. It took some getting used to because this was a very different pace from the Americans with their frantic, driven, nonstop activity, but they took to heart the old adage "When in Rome, do as the Romans do" and learned how pleasant gearing down could be.

Kat and Bob spent many happy hours hiking in the surrounding flower-covered foothills. During their exploring, they discovered an old, abandoned white church that became symbolic of the steadfast relationship they shared. When the couple stopped to rest, they spread a blanket and picnicked on crusty rolls with sweet butter, ate salami, and drank hearty Chianti. They thrived in the glory of a love that they considered God ordained, growing closer over a year's time. So when Kat's stepfather was transferred back to the States, they promised to write—and meant it.

After Bob transferred back to the States, the two met at a preagreed-upon location for a reunion. Bob stooped onto one knee and said, "Make me the happiest man on the planet. Be my wife."

Kat looked at those warm brown eyes and thought of the honesty, kindness, and gentleness behind them. "Yes" followed by "Yippee" burst from her mouth as she sailed into his arm. In the years to come, they would recall this complete, unconditional commitment on the part of both of them, and it would singularly carry them through some of the hardest times—those times that every marriage must weather, or perish.

They were married in a small Methodist church on McCord Air Base in Tacoma, Washington, enjoying a modest ceremony in the company of their families only. Kat's five stepbrothers were there and brought their devilish streaks and a plan to send off the newlyweds in a way they would not soon forget.

First, they contrived to make certain Bob was completely wasted for the honeymoon night. They fed him one glass of champagne after another. "To your happiness" they toasted, coercing him to finish his drink and filling up his glass again.

Meanwhile, Kat's brother Gerald, an electronic genius by any standards, had his way with the couple's vintage Karmann Ghia. He attached the ignition to the horn, thinking it would be hilarious for the horn to blare the entire time the car ran. But Gerald was just getting started. *Wouldn't it be cool,* he thought, *if the windshield wipers were wired to the lights?* If the lights were on, the windshield wipers wouldn't work. You could have one or the other but not both. Of course, Tacoma is famous for almost-daily showers in season, April 25 being no drier than most other spring days. The guys felt obligated to tie cans on the back bumper for tradition's sake, an oldie but a goody all the same. Also, for good measure, since the reception took place on an extremely conservative air base, they designed a big duct-taped swastika on the back of the vehicle, certain that it would get the attention of the residents in base housing—maybe even the base commander. The pièce de résistance, though, was chaining the back bumper of the Karmann Ghia securely to the carport. That seemed like a good idea at the time, so brother Larry fixed them up.

The newlyweds readied themselves to leave the reception to celebrate their first night as man and wife in a shower of rice and cheers. Bob was wobbly kneed but made it to the Karmann Ghia; he stepped in and turned on the ignition. The horn blared at full blast. He tapped the horn a couple of times with a confused look on his face to no avail. He turned on the windshield wiper; the lights went off. He turned on the lights; the wipers went off. He gave up and put the car in drive and began to creep forward but found that the car met with resistance. In his champagne-influenced judgment, he gunned the motor, creeping forward until finally breaking free. He looked back to find that one of Kat's funnier brothers had chained the back bumper of the Karmann Ghia to the carport. Where the carport used to stand now stood a pile of rubble. *Good one, boys,* he thought. The Karmann Ghia was quite a spectacle that day as the newlyweds clamored through base housing with the horn blaring, an obnoxious swastika being sported on the back, the headlights flashing on and off, the cans rattling, and a chain with a wooden slat from the carport dragging nosily behind.

Chapter II

MEET BABETTE

Their first air force assignment as a married couple was March AFB in Edgemont, California, where Bob was stationed as an air traffic controller. He had the experience under his belt from his previous assignment, but beyond that, he had a natural aptitude for the job. It takes a special kind of person with a cool head to be an air traffic controller, where planes come out of nowhere and human lives are at stake. He balanced the air traffic effortlessly with a focus that could only be described as gifted. This innate ability earned him well-deserved respect from his crew and the nickname the Rock.

The two settled into a one-bedroom apartment just outside the back entrance of March Air Force Base along with many other just-starting-out air force families. The apartment was small, only one bedroom and one bath, with a balcony of sorts through the sliding glass doors off the kitchen. At that time, March AFB was home to the Strategic Air Command's Twenty-Second Bombardment Wing that flew B-52 bombers and KC-135 Stratotankers. While the thundering sound of the planes taking off and landing was an irritating constant, the apartment was conveniently located just three miles from the control tower's parking lot, and the price was right. In truth, the newlyweds were so happy to have their first place together it could have been a tent in the Sahara desert, and they wouldn't have cared.

Air traffic controllers work rotating shifts. Like pilots, there are laws in place limiting the number of hours worked in a twenty-four-hour period as well as required extended-rest periods over a seven-day period. The idea is to make certain personnel are fresh to make crucial decisions. The rotating shift meant that Bob's days off would change each week. One week his free days might be Monday and Tuesday, and the next week might be Sunday and Monday, etc. That constantly rotating shift made it difficult but he managed to enroll in the local community college and work toward a good education, so important to both of them.

At work, Bob always parked in an outlying parking lot located a bit more than a mile from the tower. He used the time hiking to the tower to "get in the zone" because the high stress of the job could be daunting. After his shift, Bob would defuse on the walk back by thinking of his bride, who was, depending on the day and time, either in school at Riverside Community College or at the Petite Sophisticate, an upscale dress shop where she worked as assistant manager.

One Saturday morning, on his end-of-shift walk back to the parking lot, Bob was surprised to hear the faint mewing of puppies. He stopped and listened intently, tracing the sound to the bank of the small lake bordering the east side of the runway. There, to his dismay, he saw a young man, twenty to twenty-five years of age, holding a drenched gunnysack that he was purposely dunking in the water. It was obvious that the sack contained small struggling animals and that the man was in the process of drowning them. Bob charged without thinking and confronted the man menacingly. "What are you doing?"

The man stood and took a defensive posture. "Mind your own business. I can't take care of them. These are my pups, and I'll do what I want." After which, the man took a threatening step forward. The act of brutally harming a litter of defenseless puppies was so cowardly, foreign, and repulsive to Bob that he reacted on a basic human level and charged the man. The man dropped the soggy bag and ran.

Bob quickly untied the sack and removed one small lifeless body after another, heartsick to find the beautiful animals still. He shook each puppy, hoping for a response as he laid their four bodies at his feet, their tiny tongues protruding. As he shook the fifth puppy, he was heartened to detect a response; the tiny baby's sides began laboring to suck in breath. Bob put the puppy in his coat pocket and sprinted to his car, wishing the worst kind of fate on the puppy murderer. He climbed into his car, slammed it into drive, and sped to the small apartment that he and Kat had made their home. Sitting in the parking lot of the apartment, Bob carefully examined the puppy to be certain that he was not taking a dead animal to his beloved bride. He could tell that while it was in trouble, it continued bravely to suck oxygen into its lungs. He thought it looked somewhat improved from its original state when he found it. He took a deep breath and opened the door. It was likely going to be a long night.

When Bob opened the door to the second-floor apartment, he surveyed the small, brightly decorated room. It was furnished sparsely with a couch purchased from friends who relocated, some worn chairs, and a hand-me-down bed in the bedroom that was given to them by Kat's parents. Their kitchen table was a low Kyoto-style table that Bob had made from scrap lumber. The couple used pillows to sit on the floor to take their meals. The apartment was scrupulously clean, and while sparsely furnished, the couple was proud of their home.

Bob found Kat lounging with a book in her hand on the secondhand sofa. He called to her, "Kat, you would not believe what I just saw. I saw some heathen drowning a litter of puppies down by the runway."

As a confirmed animal lover, she was beside herself with righteous anger. As she railed at the cruelty of the act, she looked up to see Bob cradling a tiny, furry puppy that was making an effort to mew. It was no surprise to Bob to see his wife grasp the animal and wrap it in a towel. She located a heating pad and placed the shivering puppy on the surface. Kat dashed to a neighbor's apartment to borrow a doll's baby bottle and coaxed the puppy to suckle warm milk. The puppy struggled the whole night long, and no one slept. About three o'clock, the puppy rallied, sleeping more easily. The next morning, it weakly mewed, and the decision was made that it be taken directly to a vet.

Kat located a vet who practiced in Edgemont only a couple of miles from the apartment. When she got there, she barged in, crying and relating the story of the cretin who had drowned the other puppies. She pleaded with the vet that this one be saved. As he examined the puppy, he warned Kat that he could make no guarantee. The puppy, he said, was a female and likely about three days old. The umbilical cord was still attached. Very likely the puppy had been suckled by the mother dog some because it was still hydrated, which improved its odds of survival.

He added that, judging by its features, his best guess was that it belonged to a breed known as Shih Tzu. As adults, they weighed in at about twelve to fifteen pounds, with short legs and very silky, almost-humanlike hair that grew quite long. The puppy had floppy tan ears with a blaze of white on her forehead and the tip of her tail, relatively no snout, a decided under bite, and a flat face almost like a persian cat. In proportion to her short body, the tail was long, and it curled up so as to lie on her back. As Kat held the puppy for the vet to examine, its tiny pink tongue appeared briefly and licked Kat on the back of the hand. Kat thought to herself that it was absolutely the cutest puppy she had ever seen. As the vet completed his examination, he cautioned to Kat that the chances for the puppy's survival were remote and allowed that newborn puppies went south even under the best of circumstances, which clearly this was not. As Kat stroked the pup's tiny flat face, her maternal instinct blossomed. The vet charged her for a proper feeding bottle and something called Esbilac that was milk formulated specifically for puppy consumption. As she paid the bill, she held the puppy under her chin and said with determination, "Oh yeah, it's on."

The next week was touch and go. Kat called in sick to work and skipped her college classes, concentrating instead on saving the fragile little puppy. She fed her every two hours and used a warm, soft cloth to mimic a mother dog stimulating the infant to urinate and defecate because she was too young to do so on her own. She hoped it wasn't her imagination but thought she detected improvement. The puppy began to suckle with more vigor, and if Kat slipped that two-hour deadline to feed, the pup soon began putting up an awful fuss. "*Mew, mew, mew,*" it cried indignantly. Kat allowed herself to hope. She felt it unwise to name the puppy because it could still slide from this world as easily as it might stay, thereby breaking her heart, so she called it simply Baby. Eventually, this morphed into Babette, and against her will, the puppy was named.

At three weeks, Babette opened her eyes, first one eye and then the other. Kat gazed with delight into Babette's face. She adored the flat nose; the long, long eyelashes (the entire length of the little face); and the evident intelligence of the puppy. *Odd,* she thought to herself. *She almost seems to be scrutinizing me.*

As Babette grew, she would recognize Kat's voice as she entered a room and waddle toward her, yapping excitedly. The family became inseparable. Babette slept in bed with Bob and Kat, taking her share of the bed out of the middle, and had to be in the same room, regardless if that room was the kitchen or the bathroom. Walking became hazardous because wherever a step was taken, Babette was sure to be there. In the evening, she would sit beside Bob while he watched TV with one paw placed possessively on his leg. Babette was convinced Bob belonged to her. Those times the couple left Babette in the apartment alone, they were given feedback by the neighbors in no uncertain terms. "That pup cried the whole time you were gone."

As Babette grew, so did her appeal. Nothing is as adorable as a puppy to begin with, but Babette was irresistible: an active ball of fur with two round button eyes. When she walked, she had that waddle that was exaggerated when she scampered. She would grasp a chew toy, shake it with mock ferocity, and throw it for all she was worth so that she might chase it down. With the aid of a scrap of chicken, soon she was returning the item, and if the planets were all aligned just so, sometimes she would release it willingly. She was a rock star wherever she went; people crowded around her to stroke her fur or admire her waddle.

By the age of nine weeks, the matter of obedience training was discussed. Babette was extremely bright but seemed to think outside the box from other dogs. First on the list of any good dog owner's goals is housebreaking. Kat had read an article about teaching a dog to ring a cowbell dangled on a rope from the front doorknob when it needed to go out to relieve itself. Since the couple was living in a second-floor apartment where a doggy door was not feasible, this method seemed a good idea. So the cowbell was purchased and hung on the doorknob, and Babette was introduced to the device. Kat raised Babette's paw and assisted it to strike the bell. Immediately after striking the bell, Babette was given a piece of chicken, and the love affair with the bell was born. Babette promptly rang the bell with her small paw and turned expectantly to Kat. And sure enough, there was a piece of chicken for her efforts, and moreover, she was taken on a walk. Magic, that bell. What could be better to a little dog? Just as soon as the walk was over and Babette was back in the apartment, she made a beeline for the bell. She began pawing the bell then demanding her chicken. It got to the point that it sounded like a church service in the apartment as Babette's frustration grew. She was pretty sure that if she just rang that bell loudly enough that a scrap of chicken would appear. This can be said to be an example of the best-laid plans not panning out exactly as expected. Eventually, the bell had to go so the family could sleep again.

Still the question of training loomed. The couple turned to the local pet store for classes and enrolled her in an obedience/socialization class. Quickly Babette grew to recognize the location of the pet store and all the great fun to be had there, and when the car pulled up for the group lesson, Babette became so excited that she practically vibrated. Once the car parked, she scurried out the door, ready for class. Babette loved the other dogs and all the other owners, so she made certain to greet each pet and especially their owners personally in case they wanted to pick her up to pet her or give her a tummy rub. She assimilated all the tasks easily. Basic obedience included the orders "Sit," "Lay," "Stay," "Heel," and something known as "Leave it." The instructor explained that "Leave it" was an important command so the animal could be protected against accidental poisoning if it found something on a walk and attempted to eat it. The procedure went like this: When the animal was observed stooping to eat something questionable, the owner was to holler, "Leave it." When the dog dutifully spat out the substance, the obedience was rewarded with a treat. You guessed it: a piece of chicken. Babette would do a back flip for a piece of chicken, and if those were the stakes, well, you could count her in.

During one of the practice walks in the local park, the command came in handy. As they walked along, Babette found a castor bean pod. It is a wonder that such a plant would be found in a park where children and dogs played because it is deathly toxic, but nevertheless, there it was. Babette mouthed the castor bean pod, and Kat shouted, "Leave it." Babette obeyed the command she had learned in class and spat out the offending, poisonous pod. Lo and behold, she received a tasty morsel of chicken. You could almost see the wheels churning in her tiny mind. From that day forward, Babette would hit that park and aggressively seek out castor bean pods. She would pick one up in her mouth, look to Kat, then after hearing "Leave it," she would drop it and wait expectantly for her chicken reward. That worked so well she would seek out another castor bean pod. Again, not everything is as ideal in practice as it appears at face value. It took months to discourage Babette from hunting castor bean pods in the park.

Babette was the darling of the apartment complex and had no shortage of people willing to dog sit. As a consequence, she was fortunate to develop amazing socialization skills with a high regard for people. She traveled everywhere and left all she touched better for having stroked her fur or played the never-ending game of fetch Babette-style. The family settled in to a period of peace and happiness with the little dog cementing the deal.

Chapter III

ESMERALDA AND BABETTE—BEST FRIENDS

One of the Johnny-on-the spot dog sitters in the apartment complex was a seven-year-old African American child named Esmeralda. She was a beautiful girl though shy and tiny for her age and with delicate features and a soft, almost-melodic voice. She suffered from a seizure disorder known as epilepsy that had been diagnosed when she was three years old. She was on medication for the condition, but there were frequent breakthrough seizures—a couple of which had occurred at school, earning her the cruel taunt of "Shaker Baby pees her pants." She was often lonely as her unfortunate condition was scary to the children, causing them to ostracize her—a travesty because the girl was one in a million with her winning smile and a heart of gold.

Each day, Esmeralda would race home from school and seek out Babette with open arms. She would grin in delight when she saw her, and the two would carry on as though they had not seen each other for a year. Babette would stage a dance that came to be known in the complex as Do the Babette. She would prance on one foot and then the other, making a circle with her movement. Her head would bob from side to side with her fluffy behind waving in the opposite direction and her tail wagging a mile a minute, and amazingly, she would smile a doggy grin and close one eye in a wink. Anyone who saw Babette in action had to laugh. Soon Esmeralda learned to emulate the cheerful dance, and people in the apartment complex would leave their apartments just to witness this simple act of unrestrained joy.

Esmeralda often spent the afternoons in Babette's company, whereupon they played fetch, watched TV together, or Babette would have the privilege of modeling doll clothes and being pushed about the block in a doll stroller. To her credit, even though Babette took a dim view of the doll clothes, she was a good sport and tolerated them. The little pink doll stroller though, that she loved. She would sit up in the front of the stroller, interacting with everyone who passed by certain that they were put on this earth to pet her. The two made a comical sight: Esmeralda pushing the stroller proudly and Babette with her tongue lolling and dressed with a bib, a doll's diaper, and a pacifier strung around her neck on a pink ribbon.

Kat called Esmeralda one afternoon and asked if she could puppy sit because Kat had a lab scheduled for one of her nursing classes. Esmeralda was thrilled, and thirty seconds from the phone call's ending, she pounded on the front door of Kat's apartment. When Kat opened the door, both Babette and Esmeralda broke into the dance, cavorting with wild abandon. Esmeralda chanted "Do the Babette, do the Babette" as she and the dog in unison hopped from foot to foot with their heads bobbing one way and their tails in the opposite direction, sporting winks and smiles on their faces as large as the summer sky. The girl scooped the tiny, wiggling puppy into her arms, where Babette licked Esmeralda's face until it was wet. Eventually, Kat got the two calm enough to put on the leash, give Esmeralda Babette's water bottle and food, and escort the two to Esmeralda's downstairs apartment.

Esmeralda played the afternoon with Babette but seemed subdued. The two even had a nap together in the bottom bunk bed in the playroom, Babette curled tightly against Esmeralda's belly and cuddled in her arms. After rising from the nap, Esmeralda appeared listless and refused to eat though she fed Babette some kibble.

An hour later, Babette sought out Esmeralda's mother and began racing in a circle and whimpering. She pranced from one foot to the other and whined as if she were having a heart attack. "What's the matter, Babette?" Esmeralda's mother asked. "Potty time?" She stood and reached for Babette, intending to take her outside, but Babette evaded her grasp and scampered down the hallway toward the playroom door. Esmeralda's mother followed Babette, calling to her softly all the while, "What's the matter, sweetie? What's wrong?" But Babette continued to make her way to the toy room, whining loudly. Esmeralda's mother followed Babette at last entering the toy room. She surveyed the toy-strewn room and was surprised to find Esmeralda on the top bunk and sitting upright and stiffly staring forward. "Esmeralda, Esmeralda." Her mother scaled the bunk and gently shook the child, but there was no response.

Then Esmeralda's small body quaked with a writhing motion, the child's eyes rolled up in her head, and she lost her urine. Her mother restrained Esmeralda from the edge of the top bunk and waited for the seizure to abate. Babette could be seen on the floor watching intently, making no sound but in obvious distress. Esmeralda convulsed for about three minutes then gradually awoke as if from a sleep, blinking and asking her mother, "What happened?" Her mother explained that she had a dilly of a seizure and repeated the hard-and-fast rule that Esmeralda was not to be in the top bunk for any reason. It was only for company's use during sleepovers specifically because of this eventuality. Then Esmeralda's mom peered over the top bunk's edge to look at Babette with a look of astonishment on her face. She recalled Babette's urgent actions that led her to the playroom. Had Babette somehow known that Esmeralda would have a seizure?

Over time, this ability of Babette to predict Esmeralda's seizures was proven again and again. It was always the same behavior, the prancing and low whining, though Esmeralda's mother was moved into immediate action on these other occasions, confident of Babette's reliability.

There was the time Esmeralda and Babette had gone on a stroller adventure around the block with Babette dressed to the nines in a hat, a bib, and a doll's diaper. In almost no time, Babette returned to the apartment, scratching frantically at the front door. When Esmeralda's mother answered the door, she found Babette in a sun bonnet, with a doll's diaper dragging behind her on one leg, prancing from one foot to the other and whining. She sped out the door with the little dog flicking off the diaper and leading the way to find Esmeralda sitting in the middle of the street and stiffly staring forward. Her mother arrived in time to pull Esmeralda from the street before the seizure occurred, but had it not been for Babette, what kind of peril might the child have faced?

The third time was the most extraordinary. Kat and Babette were sitting in the fenced area where the community pool was. They were talking and gossiping with the neighbors, their dogs, and their preschool children. Out of the blue, Babette began barking and whining. She was inconsolable, so eventually, Kat gave up and opened the gate to the fenced pool to take Babette home. Babette slipped off her leash and collar; bolted out of the gate, running for all her short legs would carry her; and ended up at Esmeralda's apartment where she scratched until Esmeralda's mother opened the door.

As soon as she saw Babette's familiar behavior, Esmeralda's mother reacted. Esmeralda was not home; she was at school. She grabbed her car keys, drove to the March AFB Elementary School, and fled to Esmeralda's classroom. She burst into the classroom, but the children were at recess. Esmeralda's mother searched the playground desperately to finally find Esmeralda at the top of the slide, a place she was expressly forbidden to be, staring stiffly ahead and the other children scolding, "Slide down, Esmeralda. We're waiting." The ladder to the top of the slide was occupied by children, so Esmeralda's mother crawled up the slide from the front, slipping once, and arrived to gather Esmeralda in her arms just in time as the child lost consciousness and began the tonic-clonic seizing. Her mother brought her to safety amazingly thanks to Babette.

Esmeralda's family called themselves believers. They had witnessed Babette's ability to predict an impending seizure, and they would not be persuaded otherwise. Any time they recounted the events to friends, they were met with the same skeptical expression and a condescending "Right." So the family, with Kat's help, decided to research this kind of canine phenomena online to see if there was any documentation of such a thing happening.

They discovered many anecdotal incidents of dogs predicting impending seizures. Owners recounted tales of their dogs alerting them as much as forty-five minutes prior to the onset of the actual symptoms, giving them the opportunity to reach a safe venue or enlist help. The method used by the dog to alert their owners was as individual as the dog itself. Pawing, whining, circling, and making pointed and close eye contact are all cited as witnessed acts exhibited by dogs that bought their owners time to avoid catastrophe. There is even documentation of dogs affording the seizure patients protection during the seizures by lying down beside the person or even on top of them to prevent injury.

The scientific community heeded these accounts and began the study of dogs able to anticipate seizures in earnest. There's no disagreement that canines have a sense of smell touted to surpass our own by as much as one hundred thousand times. The speculation is that the animal is able to recognize subtle biochemical changes in the bloodstream with their heightened olfactory nerves that herald an imminent seizure.

Another popular theory is that an animal can perceptively identify behavioral changes that predict a seizure. The dog may recognize certain patterns of behavior that warn of an impending seizure—behavior like Esmeralda's stiffness, for example.

Another proposed explanation is that dogs can identify out-of-the-ordinary autonomic responses that accompany seizures. Sweating profusely or hyperventilating may be detected by dogs prior to the actual event signaling the onset of a seizure. It has been suggested that these autonomic responses may possibly result in a sort of "aura" that could be a red flag indicating an imminent seizure that's visible to dogs only.

After researching other accounts of dogs accurately able to detect an imminent seizure, the family felt vindicated in believing in Babette's ability to do so. After all, it wasn't as if Babette invented this astonishing talent; the heroic actions of many other dogs served as living proof of this phenomena.

But what of the instance when Esmeralda was at school and Babette was at the apartment complex, both separated minimally by five miles? Certainly, any odor emitted by a chemical marker could not be smelled from that distance. Or could it? But if so, what could that mean? Could a dog truly detect such an odor from a distance of five miles? They collaborated by visiting each of the established theories, but nothing seemed to quite fit. No one could venture a guess except to say that the child and the dog had a strong, significant emotional bond that might have contributed to the prediction. The families carefully avoided recounting this incidence to people because they could find no similar incident documented to offer as evidence but secretly were certain that they had been privilege to something very, very special.

When the time came for Kat and Bob to relocate, Esmeralda tearfully said good-bye to Babette, hugging her closely. She told the puppy that they would be together again so Babette was not to cry, but Esmeralda herself shed large tears. To lose that cocoon of safety and love would leave a large hole in Esmeralda's heart as Babette had been a good and maybe her only friend.

Her parents could not bear the desolate little girl's loneliness. Kat gave them the name of a service dog organization, Service Dogs for Independence, who referred them to an organization that trained specifically seizure response dogs—service dogs trained to detect seizures.

They contacted the organization to discuss obtaining a service/response dog and were delighted with what they found. They were told some interesting facts about seizure response dogs. Of all the dogs evaluated, approximately only 15 percent of the dogs were trainable to detect seizures. This ability had to be innate—either they had it or they didn't. Also, the dog had to be in the company of their new owners for around six months to become sufficiently intimately acquainted with their new owners before the training could be counted on to kick in with any accuracy.

A trained seizure response dog meant a brand-new world for persons suffering from epilepsy. Much of the terror of a seizure has to do with the suddenness and unpredictability of the condition. This has a sizeable impact on the person's quality of life. For example, is it safe to drive? Can this person go shopping alone without fear? Go swimming? Even walking across the street or around the block is an act filled with danger if a seizure strikes. Many of us take for granted these simple pleasures that are just dreams for a seizure patient.

These seizure response dogs are trained in other aspects of care for their owners, predicting the seizure being only one important service. Some of the tasks that a seizure response dog is trained to accomplish are protecting the person against injury, getting help, not interfering with EMS personnel if summoned, situating their owners so their airways are not blocked, using a 911-alert system, and guarding their owners during the drowsy period after the seizure.

Esmeralda's family knew from firsthand experience that the prediction of a seizure by a dog is a fact in the realm of reality. They had witnessed Babette do it. They petitioned to receive a seizure response dog and were told they actually had a trained poodle-shih tzu mix available. It resembled Babette in that it was fluffy and with a flat snout and long lashes but was very different in coloring: black and white with shades of gray. Esmeralda named her new dog Babette.

Chapter IV

BABETTE AND MARGARET

The next air force assignment would be to Phoenix, Arizona, but before relocating, the couple planned a long-overdue visit to Bob's folks in Johnstown, Pennsylvania. The family bid their friends in the complex good-bye, packed their household goods, and caught a United flight out of the Seattle Airport.

They flew into Pittsburgh International Airport, rented a car, and anxiously traveled the hour-and-a-half trip to Johnstown. The lush, hilly landscape contrasted sharply with Southern California's mostly desert terrain from whence they came. They used the time to talk about Bob's family, giving Kat some family history.

Bob was named in honor of his father, Robert Senior. Robert Senior was of Mennonite descent and reflected that Puritanical value from which he was raised. He was quiet, stern, frugal, and did not participate in small talk or what he considered to be frivolous pursuits. He insisted that his children be unquestionably moral and with core values, such as honesty, reliability, and charity. In short, he insisted on arming his children with a sound moral compass with which to venture out in life. He ruled his family firmly from a patriarchal position.

Bob Senior's greatest ambition in life had been to serve his country when young because he believed that every man owed and must pay back this debt of patriotism for his freedom and education. That his eyesight was so poor that he was rejected from service when he tried to enlist was one of his deepest sorrows. It gave his father a great deal of happiness when Bob Junior enlisted in the air force, paying the debt that had been denied Bob Senior.

His mother, Margaret, was as opposite to Bob Senior as Kat was to Bob Junior. She was a second-generation Yugoslavian immigrant still steeped in old-world traditions and speaking Croatian within the confines of the family. Bob Junior and his sister Debbie took after her side of the family, and the three could have looked like triplets at different stages of their lives; they resembled each other so strongly. Margaret was a wise and intelligent woman able to zip through the *New York Times* crossword puzzle at record speed; no language confusion there. She was also a devoted mother lion where her cubs were concerned. She had not seen Bob Junior since he had enlisted, and that day, she rejoiced to have this family reunion. She would see to it that this was an event to remember.

When the couple entered Bob's childhood home, they found at least thirty people milling about in attendance to welcome Bob home. Tempting aromas filled the room. There were covered dishes and snacks on every surface in the kitchen and living room—delicacies Kat had not tasted before: pierogi, pigs in a blanket, *halupki*, fried cabbage, and little cakes filled with frosting that they called gobs that Kat was delirious about.

Bob introduced Kat to so many relatives that she could not keep them straight. They were universally warm and friendly, welcoming Kat with affection. His little sisters accepted her to the family with open arms. Debbie, the older of the two sisters, looked like a younger, feminine, petite Bob. She had the same long lashes framing the same inquisitive brown eyes, the same full lips, and the same coloring. His baby sister, April, was sixteen years his junior. She had light-brown hair, favored their father more than Margaret, and was lovely with the grace and confidence of German royalty. The three siblings had a close emotional bond. While they teased each other without mercy, they were fiercely devoted.

Bob pointed out another of his favorite relatives—an Aunt Jenny. He confided to Kat, "She used to hold me down when I was little and spit in my mouth." They embraced with family members as the chaos and confusion of a huge family reunion waged.

Of course, Babette was the belle of the ball. She was handed from one person to the next to be petted. The children were delighted, and Babette took the stage and strutted and preened and performed—not in the least intimidated. When she felt Babette was comfortable enough, Kat showed off Babette's repertoire of tricks—which included the standard "Sit," "Lay," "Stay," and "Fetch"—and she even pulled out a more elaborate one. Kat got Babette's attention and said, "Babette, Go find Daddy and give Daddy a kiss." Off she scampered like someone had lit her tail on fire. When she located Bob, she flew into his arms, with him fending her off in mock indignation. She licked his face until it dripped dog saliva, and his relatives roared.

It was just after that when Bob's mother reached down to pick her up. Babette looked up and froze. When Margaret extended her hand to her, Babette recoiled and howled. This was a baffling new development. Never before had Babette howled, and it was so obviously directed at Margaret. Babette refused the extended hand and ran to Bob, ducking under his arm and hiding in his lap. What could be the problem? Bob tried to reassure her and hand her to his mother, but she wriggled out of his grasp and began barking incessantly. At last, Bob and his mother shrugged, gave up trying to encourage Babette to be sociable, and went on with the party. Babette too seemed to forget her misgivings and worked the crowd, chasing balls and getting handheld treats from everyone. But when Margaret would enter the room, Babette would halt whatever she was doing, stand stock-still, and glare at Margaret, howling if she came close.

Babette had one weakness—chicken. Margaret was determined to win over the dog, and once she discovered that Babette could not under any circumstances resist a piece of chicken, she knew she had her. She would carry a scrap of chicken in her pocket and offer it to Babette as a peace offering. Babette wasn't about to turn down chicken, but she would take it grudgingly and refuse to be picked up. You could see that regardless of her obsession for chicken, she just wouldn't warm up to Margaret, chicken or no.

Finally, the abundant offer of chicken overrode whatever issues Babette had been harboring, and on the third day of the visit, Margaret succeeded in picking her up. She petted her and spoke kindly to her. At last, she cuddled her to her chest. Babette began squirming and hyperventilating. She tried to escape, but Margaret persevered, pulling out all stops where chicken was concerned. Babette struggled against her hold and refused the chicken morsels, whereupon she began gently scratching at Margaret's left chest repeatedly. Then she began howling again, so distraught that she was beside herself. Margaret set her on the floor, conceding the loss of the battle but not the war. She would continue the entire visit to try to establish a truce between herself and Babette. After much chicken and patience, Babette, who always loved everyone, rested tentatively in Margaret's lap, still uneasy. Then an odd thing happened. Babette stood on her short legs, placed one paw on either side of Margaret's neck, and seemed to stare intently into Margaret's face for a long time. She licked Margaret's cheek with her smooth pink tongue. Then she leaned down and nipped gently at Margaret's left breast in such a knowing and pointed fashion that it caused the hair on the back of Margaret's neck to stand up straight.

At the end of the day, Margaret cleaned the downstairs—straightening pillows, sweeping, and throwing away half-empty soda cans. She bent to retrieve one of Babette's tennis balls before someone stepped on it and fell and then reflected on the odd interaction. As she recalled Babette's actions and pondered Babette's mysterious dislike for her, she absentmindedly placed her hand on the spot where Babette had nipped.

Wait! There was a lump. She gingerly mapped the size and shape. It was about two inches in diameter and reminded her of what a wad of chewing gum would feel like if it had been dropped on a floor and someone accidentally had stepped on it. It was more a mass than a lump and felt as though it was stuck to the chest wall. She shivered as the first stirring of fear reached its tendrils to her heart.

She scheduled an appointment with her family physician, Dr. Osgood, the doctor that had delivered her children and taken care of their family for twenty-five years. He did a breast exam and was notably alarmed. He scheduled a sonogram, a needle biopsy, and a follow-up appointment with Margaret to review the results.

After the sonogram, Margaret waited in dread. Her appointment to follow up was scheduled two weeks from the sonogram, but she was called the same day and scheduled to meet with her doctor the next. The apprehension she felt in the pit of her stomach was actually the realization that she was in for the fight of her life.

The next day, she sat in Dr. Osgood's office flanked by her two daughters tensely awaiting his arrival. He walked in with a grim demeanor. "I'm sorry, Margaret," he said with sadness. "It's breast cancer. It's an aggressive type, and it's in its third stage. When I did the exam, I could tell there was lymph-node involvement. That's the bad news. Now the good news: I believe there is an excellent prognosis. Provided you undergo an immediate mastectomy with lymph-node removal, I believe you can beat it. You've dodged a bullet, Margaret, though if this had been diagnosed as little as six months from now, you would have had very little hope to survive."

Margaret felt like she had taken that bullet in the stomach. She endeavored to breathe normally and, above all, resist breaking down. Her two daughters were there on either side of her, each sobbing and clinging to her. She said to herself, *OK, Margaret. Show your girls the courage of a real woman. You are still these young women's mother and have the job to teach them how to face this kind of crisis. After all is said and done, a mother's job to guide her children far from ends when they reach adulthood. If you are a parent worth your salt, you teach your children how to grow old, how to go through the change, and how to die. These may be the most important teachings of all, and this may be your only chance to do it.*

In the days and weeks that followed, Margaret was like two different people. There was the woman that interacted with her stricken family. That woman went to her mastectomy wearing a smile on her face to comfort her grieving loved ones. She was the woman who stared down chemotherapy with a feigned indifference. That woman shored up her family, giving them hope and assuring them that everything would be fine—that God would carry her through healthy to the other side. She felt strongly that if she were to have to leave this world, she would do so with dignity—not like some sniveling coward that didn't have the decency to be grateful for all the wonderful blessings that had been hers in her life.

Then there was this other woman who, in the terrifying wee hours of the night, thought of the breast-cancer diagnosis as a death sentence. It was that woman who felt adamant about spending quiet quality time with each of her children. The one thing she would regret was if she died without saying those things that needed to be said. She vowed to begin the next day because who really knew what time was left?

The next morning, she called Debbie and asked her over for lunch. Debbie never hesitated for an instant. All she said was "What time?" She called in sick to work and stopped to buy a loaf of Margaret's favorite rye bread on her way over. When she arrived, Margaret met her at the door and hugged her with a spontaneity and warmth that too often get lost when interacting with adult children. As they ate a simple meal of cold roast-beef sandwiches on the rye bread that Debbie brought and homemade coleslaw, Margaret told Debbie how much she reminded her of herself. She called her smart and told her that she admired and respected her for the person she was. They spoke of times in the past, both the good times and those that were difficult. Margaret told Debbie of the time that it was Debbie's turn to lead grace at the supper table when she was three years old. Her prayer started like this: "Dear God, food is good. Germs are bad," with the family bursting to keep a straight face. And in the end before Debbie left, Margaret said simply, "I love you."

The next week, April was home from school with a cold, and Margaret took off work to be with her. There's nothing quite as good as having your mother around if you're feeling punk, and it didn't matter that April was in high school. Margaret made her tried-and-true remedy for that old demon that was the cold—thick chicken-noodle soup from scratch. April lounged on the couch with a red nose and in an old bathrobe, watching a sitcom. Impulsively Margaret swept April into a bear hug and held her. April was taken aback and asked suspiciously, "Mom is everything all right?" That was when the alter ego showed her face. That was the woman who assured April that everything was just peachy, the surgery was going to be a breeze, she didn't feel badly about the mastectomy, the chemo wasn't going to make *her* sick, blah, blah, blah.

Then the two sat together at the kitchen table talking while April ate her soup. "You know, honey," she said, "you were a late-in-life baby. Everyone thought we were nuts, but we were so happy and excited about another child that your father and I could think of little else. When you were born, we were ecstatic. You gave us a chance at a new life. We got to see the world through your eyes as a bright, fresh, rain-washed place. And you have been nothing but a pleasure to us. You're a good girl, you get good grades, you're president of your class, and you will go to college. I just know you'll make it through college." Margaret told April of a dream that she had recently had about April. In the dream, she saw April as a teacher, a leader in the community, and a wonderful mother. After lunch when April went back upstairs to rest, Margaret kissed her on the nose, something she used to do when she tucked her in at night.

Margaret was determined to spend quality time with each of her children. It would be tougher to have that time with Bob Junior because he was in Arizona attending school, but she wasn't going to give up. She popped for a plane ticket from Phoenix to Pittsburgh to be used on his semester break after the surgery was completed and while she was on chemotherapy. He came alone because he believed in his heart that she had summoned him to say good-bye, and he wanted to give that to her. She picked him up from the Pittsburgh Airport by herself so they could spend that driving time alone together, knowing they'd be mobbed by relatives at the house. They reached the highway and drove in silence, viewing the stately mountains that rose on either side and watching the sunlight bounce off the dancing silver river along the way. As she began, she chose her words carefully.

She explained to Bob that it was important to her that he knew just how proud of him she was and how much she loved him. Bob Junior had been influenced by Bob Senior as far as expressing feelings was concerned and had a devil of a time talking about touchy-feely things, but he gallantly rose to the occasion for Margaret's sake. He told her that he believed in her and that this cancer was no match for her and then told her quietly, "Fight like hell, Mom." It was then in the light of Bob's strength and kindness that Margaret let that other woman out—that scared, troubled one who squared off with her mortality in the pitiless night. She wept as she told him of her fear and that she didn't want to die. She mourned her disfigured body. She confided that she hated the chemotherapy that she was presently taking because it caused her intolerable nausea and she wondered what destruction it might be wrecking in her system. She vented and stole the power from the cancer by sharing it with her dear son and exposing it to the light of day. For the first time since the diagnosis, she truly felt she could see this thing to its end—whatever that might be.

Years later, the three siblings would get together to compare notes on the heart-to-heart conversations that Margaret had shared with each of them. All three recognized them as "good-bye speeches." Each said that the speech altered their lives in meaningful ways, making them aware of the beautiful but brief stay here on earth and grateful for the good things they enjoyed. They faced the world resolving to live each moment like it was their last. Also, their relationship with their mother took on a new closeness and warmth as a result.

April maintained that Margaret told her, in so many words, that she was her favorite. "Wait, wait, wait," Debbie said. "I'm her favorite. She told me I reminded her of her."

They quarreled over it, and while they reached no consensus, each woman would always believe incontrovertibly that she was her mother's favorite child. The hallmark of an excellent mother is to answer each child's needs so well that they each feel uniquely loved, even to the point that they each believe they are the favorite.

The sisters gave up debating and turned to Bob. "What did you get from Mom's good-bye talk?" they asked.

Bob thought for a moment then said, "I learned that when life deals a deadly blow, to circle the wagons and *hunker down with family*. I learned why turning to someone for help is so important. If you trust them enough to ask for their help, it gives that person permission to turn to you when they're in trouble. It taught me how to build a support system." Then he flashed that dazzling smile and said, "And I learned that I was Mom's favorite." Nice job, Margaret.

Margaret did fortunately survive surgery, convalescence, and physical therapy. In fact, she lived to become a favorite grandmother to Bob's only daughter. Certainly, you can count Margaret among the believers. She maintained that Babette knew that there was something wrong and saved Margaret's life that visit. Every Christmas from then on there was an elaborate gift involving chicken treats for Babette under the Christmas tree from Margaret.

Kat was surprised but not skeptical when Margaret told her that Babette had diagnosed her breast cancer before she was even aware there was a tumor because Kat was familiar with Babette's work. She went online to see if there was any evidence of such a thing happening. What she gleaned was nothing short of amazing.

The literature supports the premise that dogs have in the past identified cancers with inexplicable accuracy. For example, Sharon Rawlinson tells the story of her Cavalier King Charles Spaniel that made a constant nuisance of itself by continually nuzzling her left breast. She even visited her in the middle of the night, waking her by sniffing and pawing at her breast, which alerted her to see her doctor. When Sharon saw her physician, she was diagnosed with a brutal form of breast cancer that she was lucky enough to survive thanks to the early detection afforded her by her dog.

Or take the anecdotal account of Nancy Best from San Anselmo, California. She's a believer. Her dog kept sniffing her right breast, which spurred her to have her doctor evaluate her for breast cancer. It was determined that indeed there was a *small* tumor, and yes, it was malignant. The tumor was too small and too early to have been diagnosed without the heads-up warning from her dog.

Persuasively, there has been an explosion of scientific research on the subject. According to a double-blind study by Murdoch et al. (2006) that challenged dogs to identify breast cancer by smelling a patient's breath, they discovered an astonishing 88 percent sensitivity. Other subsequent studies performed on the same subject find at least a statistical significance that proves there is an innate ability of dogs to identify cancer possibly by the odors emitted from the cancer cells.

Beyond those personal stories of dogs' heroic detections of life-threatening breast cancers, there is now a devoted following in the scientific community with regard to other types of cancer identification as well. In an article published in the British medical journal *The Lancet* in 1989, a border collie-Doberman successfully alerted his master of a cancerous malignant melanoma mole on her thigh. Easily that mole could have taken her life without early identification. This account lent credibility to the notion that dogs have a legitimate diagnostic ability.

Since that time, interesting research has been conducted at Cambridge University Veterinary School in England on what has come to be known as Dognosis. Loosely defined, that term means dogs detecting a signature scent that correlates with a specific cancer. There's a collective body of evidence that shows dogs can sniff out lung cancer, prostate cancer, bladder cancer, skin cancer, and even a heart attack or an infection. Boggles the imagination!

When Kat shared her compelling research with Margaret, together they reflected on the similarity between what Sharon Rawlinson related in her story and Babette's epiphany with Margaret. They decided that there were some discrepancies that prevented the two incidents from being exactly alike. Sharon's Spaniel was a personal pet and ever in her close proximity. If the cancer cells emitted an unusual, toxic odor, the Spaniel would have been able to detect the new smell, being familiar with the baseline, normal scent. As for Babette, should it have been possible for Babette to smell cancer cells from across the room? And with the first encounter yet? In hindsight, Babette refused to get close to Margaret right from the beginning. Kat and Margaret mused that just as in the case of dogs predicting a seizure, only those dogs born with the innate ability to do so can launch a prediction successfully. Conversely, other dogs cannot do so at all. Was it possible that the ability to detect cancer cells successfully came in degrees? If some dogs were more adept at performing a given skill and some less, maybe Babette was more, uh, *gifted*, for lack of a better word? They could not pretend to guess. It was a mystery.

Chapter V

ARIZONA STATE ENGINEERING PRISON

Both Bob and Kat had struggled tirelessly to get an education. The cost of the college classes was only one obstacle, but worse was the time it took to work and go to school at the same time. Bob had learned of an opportunity provided by the air force to go to college to earn a degree provided he had completed his associate degree and qualified according to a set of criteria. He completed his A.A., applied for and was accepted to a program where he would attend college for two years and pay the air force back for the education with four additional years of service. Bob was to go to Arizona State University to receive his bachelor's degree in civil engineering. It would be two trying years of living at the subsistence level, but the payoff would be a brilliant future.

The couple embarked on their new life in Arizona. They found a small detached home with only an evaporative or swamp cooler to fend off the triple-digit heat for which Tempe, Arizona, was famous. The place was little more than a shack with peeling paint, a small cramped kitchen complete with roaches, a living area the size of a closet, one bathroom with a shower only, and one and a half bedrooms. But it was situated on a large, fenced yard only a short bike ride to the university's campus in an area of Tempe called Sin City. It was populated exclusively by dirt-poor college students, everything they had being directed at their education. It was a friendly, closely knit community though as everyone there was in the same financial boat.

The couple made fast friends with their neighbors Jennifer and Jim, who were also attending ASU and dealing with the same set of stressors. Jim was going to be a science teacher and was going to the university on the six-year plan. Both he and Jennifer had to work to stay afloat, so any time to study was a luxury, but they were determined to see it through. Jennifer worked in a marketing firm, supposedly as a secretary, but she described her job, with some bitterness, more as a gofer position. Jim manned a booth in one of the local gas stations at night, where he took money for the purchase of gas and sold pop. Jim and Jennifer endured the hardships with some resentment. Not so Kat and Bob. They saw this as a great honor and opportunity to be able to go to school and to build a future, and whatever got in their way was trivial in comparison.

Kat got a job at the university making copies, and Bob entered a brain-battering engineer program. The engineering students on campus were reputedly a boring, depressed bunch as they waded through imposing calculus and statistics classes. Studying was their only activity. The exceptions to that were such times as holidays and semester breaks when the engineering students went on "students gone wild" rampages in response to the rigorous academics. It was a release of steam they needed to keep them somewhat sane.

On one memorable occasion when the temperature soared over 115 degrees, even at 1:00 AM, the automatic irrigation system sprang to life at night in the lot where their house sat. Kat and Bob woke when they heard barking and loud, boisterous roughhousing going on in their backyard. They peeked out the window and found the entire neighborhood frolicking naked in the gushing sprinklers, with a drenched Babette leading the pack. It was a no-brainer. They joined the hoard.

Another time on a Christmas break when the couple attended a party staged at one of the local bar and grills named Uncle Albert's, the engineering students got determinably inebriated. Bob and Jim disappeared for what seemed like an inordinate amount of time. Finally, some of the male engineering students were complaining that they could not get into the bathroom. According to them, someone had passed out on the other side of the bathroom door, blocking the entrance. It didn't take long to put two plus two together. The guys had to be carried from the bathroom and loaded in the car. Those were the young and crazy days, those ASU days. Looking back, those were counted as mindlessly happy times regardless of the poverty and crushing academic load.

Chapter VI

GRETA MAKES HER DEBUT

Babette was taken everywhere the couple went: parties, shopping, and even the local A&W drive-in for dinner once a week—their big night out. The closely knit neighborhood catered to the small dog, spoiling her with treats and attention. Bob was nearing the end of his second semester at the university when Kat noticed that Babette seemed to be off her feed. She slept continually and would even vomit from time to time. Her belly seemed to be enlarging, and her teats engorged. For the entire world, Babette resembled a pregnant dog. Now, Babette had been spayed, so it was a remote possibility, but Kat had heard of strange incidents in humans where the tubal ligations failed and resulted in unplanned pregnancies, so maybe it could be true for spayed dogs as well. Who knew for sure?

A trip to the vet was scheduled. The vet agreed that all the symptoms displayed by Babette pointed to a pregnancy, but after testing her, he reassured Kat that Babette was experiencing a false pregnancy. He mentioned that it was not that unusual. In fact, he had seen it often that when one female in a pack became pregnant, another would often exhibit all the symptoms while not actually being pregnant.

It was then that Kat started dealing with similar symptoms. She felt ill and vomited up any food that she was able to force down. Meat was simply out of the question. Nothing greasy, please. Then she began calculating and discovered that she was two weeks late on her period.

"Good heavens," she told Bob, "I hope I have hepatitis." But the truth was obvious, and the pregnancy was officially diagnosed by the doctor. You are entitled to your opinion, but in Kat's mind and spooky as it may sound, it was first diagnosed by Babette.

After the doctor confirmed the pregnancy, Kat was happy and excited. She and Bob had talked about children, and both agreed that they wanted a family. It was a bit earlier than they had planned because Bob wanted to complete the engineering degree first, but Kat felt sure he would be elated to be a daddy. At least, she hoped.

Kat thought about how best to break the news to Bob. She wanted the moment to be memorable, and she wanted to surprise him but not give him a heart attack. On the way home from the doctor's office, she stopped at the Scottsdale Mall to stroll around and gather her thoughts. In an engraving shop called Forever Memories, she saw a beautiful, delicate sterling-silver baby rattle. *That's it,* she thought. She purchased the rattle, had it engraved with "To Daddy," and gift wrapped it in pink wrapping paper with blue ribbons. She made a lovely dinner with all of Bob's favorites: beef Stroganoff, brown rice, and spinach salad. Then she waited anxiously for him to come home.

Seeing the extravagant meal when he got home made him a little nervous. Rarely on their budget was there a splurge of this proportion possible. Then he saw the small wrapped gift on his dinner plate. He started calculating rapidly in his head. Birthday? No, that date was a month away. Christmas? Well, he was pretty sure he would have known that. Anniversary? He didn't think so but, in his panic, couldn't remember for certain. Darn! It must have been one of those anniversaries of the first date or first kiss or something stupid like that. He thought, *Here goes. I'll take a shot.* He got a goofy-looking grin on his face and said, "Happy anniversary, baby. The present I got for you is on order."

Kat stopped and thought for a second. What anniversary? It wasn't their anniversary. She watched him sweat and would have let him stew for a while for the fun of it, but she was too eager to share the news of the pregnancy with him. "Honestly, Bob," she said, exasperated. "This isn't our anniversary."

He was holding the gift, so Kat said, "Well, open it."

He unwrapped the gift and removed the elegant silver rattle uncertainly. He read the inscription and turned to Kat with a deer-in-the-headlights expression. "Does this mean that you are pregnant or that you want to start to work on a family?"

"Oh no," she answered. "You're busted. You are officially a daddy."

He smiled but turned an interesting shade of green. Recovering from the shock a bit, he said, "Thank you, Kat, for the best gift a woman can give her husband."

The couple reveled in the pregnancy. They read books tracking the baby's development, planned a healthy diet, and Bob reminded Kat to take her prenatal vitamins. They couldn't wait to announce the news to their parents. Bob was more excited than Kat as he called his parents then hers to share the miracle with them.

They were adamant with the obstetrician that the gender of the baby remained a secret, but for whatever reason, the couple believed it was a boy. Bob began calling the baby Beauregard as he talked to Kat's stomach—or Beau for short. Soon their circle of friends picked up on it. They would call and ask, "So how's Beau today?"

Jim had a good question. "What if it's a girl?" he asked as he stopped by in the morning to ride his bike to school with Bob. "What will you name her then?"

Bob thought for a second and said, "Oh, I've already decided if it's a girl to call her Beauweena or Beauweenie for a nickname."

Kat said a silent prayer to herself. "Please, God, let it be a boy. The kids will nickname her Teeny Weenie or something worse if we name her Beauweena."

Kat was determined to work till the end of her pregnancy, take maternity leave, and start right back on work. *That* was how a liberated woman handled pregnancy these days. *I am woman. Hear me roar. No whining for me.* She fought morning sickness and backache and suffered through work dismally. *Nine months of this, huh?* Kat mused as she opened the medicine cabinet for more TUMS.

While getting ready to go to work one morning, Kat noticed on one of her many, many pilgrimages to the bathroom that there was blood in the toilet. She had taken enough nursing classes to know that this couldn't be good. Bob had already ridden off on his bike to some tortuous engineering class. Kat lost no time and rushed to the phone to put in an emergency call to her obstetrician who apparently simply didn't take calls until nine. She dreaded the possibility of losing this baby. She remembered Bob's face when he unwrapped the tiny gift to find a rattle inside and realized they would be parents. She couldn't bear to take that away from him. As she wept, she pulled Babette into her lap, soaking her fur with tears.

At nine o'clock sharp, Kat was at the obstetrician's office, brooking no nonsense about not having an appointment. She demanded she see Dr. Wrigley and that right then would be a good time. She was fighting for her baby's life. After the exam, Dr. Wrigley shook his head sadly and said, "I've given you a shot of a hormone that should help to retain the pregnancy, but honestly, Kat, it's in God's hands. One thing for sure, your working days are over. You are confined to bed rest. That and the shot are all we can do."

Bob walked in from class to find Kat dutifully lying in bed, surrounded by used Kleenexes. She flew into his arms, telling him of the threatened miscarriage. She felt responsible as if she had failed somehow as a woman and told him she was sorry, apologizing multiple times. He assured her that nothing she did endangered the pregnancy and it was in no way her fault. When she looked up, she saw so much pain in his eyes that it crushed her. They held each other and vowed to do whatever it was they had to do and to face whatever might come standing united together.

And so it was that Kat was no longer a working woman and no longer in school, and all that womanly roaring she had planned to do was forgotten in an instant. She was homebound. Babette and she adopted a peaceful routine. Life took on a different, more sedate complexion. If Babette was protective before, now she was ever-constantly vigilant. Even when she was fed in the kitchen, she would grasp her little pink plastic dinner bowl in her mouth and transport it to wherever Kat was resting, eating in her company to keep a watchful eye on her. Kat slept with Babette on her stomach, a position Babette had recently adapted. At times, Babette evidently felt the baby move as she lay on Kat's lap, which caused her to startle. She would adapt a "play mode," bowing in the front and tail feathers waggling high in the back while barking playfully. Then she would bring her nose close to the area of the stomach where the tiny foot had just been, licking lovingly with her smooth pink tongue.

A typical day started in the morning with crackers and morning sickness, Babette in attendance at the toilet to cheer Kat on. Then it was a light breakfast and prenatal vitamins. Next was television time with Babette on Kat's lap watching *All My Children*. Soap operas were never something Kat had done in the past, but now they became a welcome diversion, causing her to regret all those caustic remarks she had directed at other women who watched such things. After lunch, they napped while the two awaited Bob's return from school even though he could devote no more than an hour or so before sequestering himself in the tiny study room for the rest of the day.

Anyone who has had the great privilege of a dog's companionship twenty-four hours a day, seven days a week knows what a spiritual experience it is to relate to a dog on this level. This beautiful, noble, loyal animal has incredible powers far beyond the ability to predict a seizure or suspect a pregnancy. Babette had the capacity to perceive Kat's needs accurately and address them successfully. The friendship and trust she offered were unconditional, and if an occasional irrational emotional outburst on Kat's part occurred, then Babette was up for the challenge. When Kat cried, Babette considered it her duty to lick the tears dry. If Kat felt depressed, Babette played the clown, tossing toys in the air to chase them down with her comical waddle. If Kat was happy, Babette was her partner in joy.

Bob was grateful for Babette's tireless companionship because this pregnant, grouchy, housebound Kat bore no true resemblance to the independent workaholic with whom he was acquainted. He could often be seen with a befuddled look on his handsome face, at a loss on how to cope with this bewildering stranger. One day, in frustration he uttered, "I didn't sign up for this." But Babette, oh, she knew. She was the willing nursemaid who could minister to any emotion deftly and gladly. He was heard to mumble to Babette at one point, "Sorry, old girl. But better you than me." To this, she merely wagged her tail.

One day after having lunch, Kat felt ill. This was nothing out of the ordinary. It turned out that pregnancy was not the glowing, life-affirming experience that all those liars had told her it would be. She had to admit it wasn't her favorite thing. But that morning, she seemed even more miserable than usual. First of all, she calculated that she spent more time urinating than all other activities combined. Other women commiserated, stating that this was a common complaint—the result of the baby lying on the bladder. But what about the ugly headache? The constant thirst? And her vision was so blurry she could barely read. Did pregnancy destroy a woman's vision? As this was Kat's first pregnancy, she reasoned these were what you get and adapted a grin-and-bear-it attitude.

She felt worse and worse as the day wore on and decided that she would try to sleep. Babette curled up around Kat's expanding tummy but could not seem to get comfortable. Eventually, the two drifted off to sleep. An hour or so later, Babette snapped awake. She pawed at Kat, but there was no response; Babette could not waken her. Babette was not to be put off and began whimpering and even barking, but Kat remained unconscious. Babette alternately howled loudly and panted. She ran out the back doggy door barking at full volume but could rouse no one as everyone living close by was at school. She frantically dug under the fence like she was possessed. It took over a half hour, and her paws were raw and bleeding at the end, but she tunneled under that fence. She stormed anyone she could find on the street, barking in a way that some interpreted as aggressive. One dog lover bent to retrieve her, but she ran just outside of his grasp then stopped, turned to face him again, and barked some more. He followed, and Babette led him on a merry chase down Spence Avenue until the two stood in front of the dilapidated house. He reached for her, and she charged into his arms, licking his face like a long-lost friend. He sought her collar and found her tag with the address confirming that this was indeed her home. He knocked at the door repeatedly, but there was no answer.

About that time, Jennifer came home from work for lunch and saw that Babette was being held by a stranger who was pounding at the Walters' front door. She inquired, "Can I help you? My friend lives there."

Babette leaped out of the stranger's arms and went into a full-blown Do the Babette caper—whirling in a circle, hopping on one foot then the other, and head bobbing one direction and back end going the other while with a wink and her best dog smile. The stranger told her that the little dog had been loose and in a panic. When Jennifer heard that Babette was loose and on her own in the neighborhood, she knew instinctively that something was wrong—very wrong. The two continued to bang at the door, but Kat did not respond. Jennifer picked up a rock and, with absolutely no hesitation, broke out the window. She went through the broken window calling Kat and ran to the bedroom. She shook Kat and called her name while trying to fend off Babette, who pounced on the bed whining and licking Kat's face. Nothing. "Call 911," she directed to the stranger urgently. "The phone is in the kitchen." They waited a tense ten minutes with Babette wailing the whole time. When the paramedics swooped in, they took a set of vitals that included blood sugar and found Kat's blood sugar to be dangerously high. The paramedics transported Kat by ambulance to the local Salt River Project Hospital. As soon as she hit the emergency room, insulin was administered, reviving Kat as if by magic.

Bob came home from school to a frantic Jennifer and an exhausted, troubled Babette. He went directly to the hospital. The doctor met him in Kat's room to reassure him. "Kat's going to be OK," he said. "She has a condition we call gestational diabetes." Blood sugar is always elevated in pregnancy, he explained to Bob; it's how the body manages to feed both the mother and the added burden of the baby, but in some cases, it gets out of hand, as it did with Kat. "She will need to take insulin during her pregnancy to keep the blood sugars at a safe level for both mother and infant. The infant's heart rate and ultrasound are normal, so we think there has been no damage. It's just a lucky thing that Kat's friend got to her when she did, or Kat would have sunk into a coma, and no question the baby would have been compromised." But Kat,

Jennifer, and the stranger who helped that morning might have said that the doctor named the wrong heroine.

Kat checked the internet to discover extensive, clear documentation verifying that dogs have displayed this unique skill to detect abnormal blood sugar levels. In fact, next time you see a service dog, there is a very good chance that the animal has been trained to monitor his/her owner's blood glucose level.

You might ask Ashley Bogdan, a thirteen-year-old girl, about her dog, Bria. In an article printed by *USA Today* about Canine Companions for Independence, Ashley relates that Bria, her diabetic-service dog, has been trained to detect unsafe blood sugar levels, both highs and lows. This is a godsend to a teenager trying to live a normal life, but even more important is the long-range benefit of keeping blood sugar levels from reaching the danger zone. Persistent high blood sugar levels damage the vessels in the eyes and kidneys as well as destroy nerves. Keeping the blood glucose levels normal may keep her off dialysis later or prevent future blindness. Low blood sugar levels are even more perilous and can mean a coma or even cost her life. How is it possible for a dog to perceive an abnormal blood glucose level, you ask? The answer is that it is one of the beautiful canine mysteries, like the way Babette had always been able to foretell a trip to the vet or the dreaded groomers. Only the canine population knows.

The pregnancy was considered high risk before because of the early spotting, but with the gestational diabetes added to the mix, Kat was now relegated to strict bed rest. Additionally, Kat was considered underweight for her five-foot-five height. She had only weighed 109 pounds when the pregnancy was diagnosed and was now steadily losing weight instead of gaining it as a result of the excessive morning sickness, something the doctor called as hyperemesis gravidarum. The doctor was worried that Kat did not have the body mass index to sustain a healthy pregnancy and even felt this could have been the cause of the early spotting. He offered an antiemetic medication to counteract her morning sickness, but Kat had seen the work of such medications, like the thalidomide nausea medication that caused babies to be born limbless. She was having none of that. Dr. Wrigley shrugged his shoulders and said, "OK, Kat. You've got to get nourishment to that baby. Then eat and eat some more, and no more vomiting."

Kat secretly stuck her tongue out at the doctor. *Spoken just like a man,* she thought. *He must think I like all this throwing up.*

Kat did everything she could to put on weight, and Bob was beside himself to help. It could have been 1:00 AM in the morning, but if Kat mentioned she could go for an Uncle Albert's pizza, Bob was out the door—only to return with the pizza and find Kat just could *not* eat the thing. This wasn't unusual. If Kat wanted a donut, he would bring home a box of doughnut holes from the Donut Hole Hut. If she thought she could actually eat some pancakes, he would make pancakes. Even though Kat's heart was in the right place, her stomach refused to cooperate. The thing was this: what to do with all the food? In their financial predicament, waste was not an option. Plus, these were high-calorie goodies seldom seen in their frugal household. So Bob did the only thing a guy could do in that situation: he ate them. At the end of the pregnancy, Kat put on nineteen pounds, and Bob put on twenty-five. His friends harassed Bob, wanting to know if it was a boy or a girl and when he was going to deliver. Bob failed to find it funny.

Kat had always found it so difficult to be inactive. The best word to describe her was *energetic,* so it was a really herculean task for her to comply with the enforced bed rest. But the threat of endangering the baby caused her to respect the recommendations of the obstetrician, and she even came to enjoy the quiet domesticity. Babette was her constant companion, and the family saw the rest of the pregnancy to eight months without further trouble.

Late in the eighth month of pregnancy, Kat experienced what she thought were gas pains. Either gas or a phenomenon she had studied in nursing school called Braxton-Hicks contractions. The body simulated these Braxton-Hicks contractions as a trial run to prepare for the main event—actual labor. Kat remained calm and patiently monitored the contractions, which persisted over three days' time and became more regular as time went by. She was skeptical about this being the time to deliver because she was still weeks too early for the projected full-term date. Of course, she was anxious to hold her newborn infant, but she wanted the baby to have every chance to be fully developed. The morning of the fourth day, before Bob had left for school, the contractions began to increase in strength and were pretty regular at ten minutes apart. When she bent over to pick up Babette, she felt a whoosh of water. She knew it was show time. She smiled at Bob and said, "Bob, honey, the baby is coming."

They had practiced for this event, were packed, had taken Lamaze classes, and knew the route to the hospital, and it was time to put it all into motion. Bob had a stricken look on his face and was notably flustered. He kept repeating "This is it! This is it!" like a mantra. But somehow the keys, which were always on a nail by the door, were not to be found. Then the suitcase flew open when he picked it up because whoever put the last item inside forgot to close it properly. To make matters more confusing, Babette was in full Do the Babette mode, barking wildly and turning in circles cheerfully. Finally, all was loaded, and the couple took off for the hospital, but it was Kat who drove.

Bob described the delivery later as "The ride of my life." Early on, they employed all the Lamaze techniques they had learned. Bob hung a picture of the two of them picnicking on a sunlit day on a beautiful California beach, which was taken when they were younger and more carefree—what they referred to as their before-baby days. Kat had selected this as the photo on which to focus as recommended in her Lamaze class. They practiced their breathing exercises. They talked excitedly of the nursery the couple had set into place in the study room, the crib bought at a yard sale that they had painted orange and stenciled frolicking yellow dogs along the edges, and the matching Tigger mobile and lamp that was waiting for their bundle of joy.

Soon though, Bob glanced up and noticed an ugly, scowling look on Kat's face. "How are you doing, honey?" he asked with the muscle in his left cheek twitching, more than a little afraid.

"Who wants to know?" she snapped.

Things went downhill from there. Kat mentioned to him that he ground his teeth in his sleep if he didn't know, that he chewed too loudly when he ate, that he had developed a gut since starting school and maybe he should cut down on the beer on the weekends, and that he was the spitting image of his father who had recently lost most of his hair. Bob tried winningly to redirect Kat to employ all those Lamaze techniques they had studied over the months, suggesting she focus on the picture on the wall. Kat mentioned divorce.

About that time, the baby crowned, bringing back a sense of purpose to everyone in the room. The doctor instructed Kat to push and steered Bob to the end of the exam table so he could witness the birth of what would be his only daughter. He handed Bob a pair of scissors to sever the umbilical cord. "We did it!" Bob exclaimed. To which Kat gave him an unfair, sour look but forgave him as soon as the nurse put the swaddled female infant on Kat's stomach.

The baby was to be named Greta, a German form of Margaret, in honor of Bob's mother, though at this stage, she looked more like Bob's father as she appeared singularly bald. Bob held Kat, and the two gazed at Greta, who seemed to look back into their loving faces intently.

She looked like Bob and Kat if they had put their features in a bag and shook them up. She would have Kat's coloring. Her downy blond hair was practically invisible; it was so light. She would be what used to be called towheaded in the old days. The stunning blue eyes were the same aquamarine color of her mother's but with long lashes, an unmistakable gift from her daddy. Her complexion was fair, which described either parent, but the shape of the nose and mouth resembled her father more than her mother. It was uncanny to see the combined features mimicked on Greta's face so identically.

Kat sensed the immortality that every child represents. Those unique features, a combination of Bob and Kat and born of their love, would go out into the world stamped on Greta's face as ever-present evidence of their devotion. Principles important to the couple would be taught to Greta, and she would be their emissary taking Bob's steadfast strength of character and Kat's embrace of life to the world. That perspective given to her at her parents' knees would also be taught to her children. The legacy would carry forward to their grandchildren and to their children after. If this wasn't a chance to influence the world, a bit of posterity if you will, what was?

She keenly felt the responsibility of the task at hand, more important than any other she had undertaken, the rearing of a valuable human being. She rubbed her palm across Greta's chest, feeling her tiny heartbeat; set her teeth; and said to herself, "Oh yeah . . . it's on."

The day Kat and Greta were discharged from the hospital, the entire neighborhood was in attendance to welcome them home. The tiny dilapidated shack was brimming wall to wall with people drinking beer, laughing, and helping Jim, who was chief barbecue chef in the backyard. Any time you have a man barbecuing, you'll have a crew of men beside him who all know how to do it just a little bit better.

"You gotta parboil the ribs," one veteran chef insisted.

Another offered, "No, man! Brining the meat first is the way to go."

Another confirmed the secret was the sauce. "The sauce needs plenty of brown sugar and Jim Beam in it."

The debate waged on, fueled by the liberal partaking of beer.

The impromptu party was a surprise to Kat as she walked in from the car. Babette was already at the door wiggling and winking vigorously in a frenzy. Kat handed their precious daughter to her papa and caressed the enthusiastic dog. Babette was then relegated to the back bedroom for her protection so as not to be stepped on or injured in the crowd in any accidental way.

The women by turns held the baby and coached Kat on how best to parent. This they considered their God-given duty as Greta was a first baby and nursing program or not, Kat was green as grass in the motherhood department. The problem was that each woman had her own philosophy, so the wisdom they were trying to impart began to degenerate into arguments. For example, do you put an infant on their back or their tummy? There were apparently whole bodies of thought on this topic as diametrically opposed as could be imagined.

One group maintained that if you put the baby on her stomach, she could suffocate or get crib death and die. The other group argued that if the baby is colicky, laying the child on their stomach is the best way to relieve gas and cure the colic. The only things that had universal agreement where the women were concerned were that breast-feeding was mandatory and that a child could not be spoiled with love—only with things.

There was a community feeling in the home as everyone celebrated the hope that a new infant brings. Bob came in from the barbecue-debate squad and found his wife. He ran his hand along her face and asked, "Are you tired?"

And she nodded. "Yes."

After the meal was completed and the women had cleaned up the dishes, Bob stood to address his friends while holding Greta with her back against his chest. It was reminiscent somehow of the opening scene of *The Lion King* as Bob beamed with fatherly pride. "We are so blessed to have these good friends," he said. "And we can't thank you enough for all your support. But my wife is tired, and we would like some time alone with the baby. So thank you all for coming. Please don't go away mad. Just go away." He passed out cigars as the crowd filed past him, clapping him on the back and exclaiming what a perfectly beautiful baby Greta was.

The party did not break up so much as move on. It could be heard waging at Jim and Jennifer's house long into the night. Happy birthday, Greta.

After the last friend left, Bob wrapped Kat in his arms and kissed her chastely on the forehead. They gathered up Greta and retired to the sanctuary and solitude of their modest bedroom. They lay Greta between them and undressed her to her diaper while they memorized her sweet tiny fingers and held her feet in their hands. They talked together and planned. They dreamed about her future and how she would look.

Then in the peace of the moment, Kat breast-fed Greta while Bob gazed on in awe. He marveled at the feelings flooding in on him. He thought how impossible it was to imagine the depth and extent of these feelings before actually experiencing the birth of a child from a loving relationship. If you were given the task of explaining to an alien or, let's say, a sixteen-year-old boy about the impact this has on a person's soul, could you satisfactorily do so? Could you persuade him to empathize with the all-encompassing gut slam of gazing into your infant's face and seeing *your* eyes except this time those eyes are as pale blue as the dawn sky? This is akin to expounding a dissertation of just what it is like to fall in love for the first time but far, far more life altering. Bob thought to himself, *If this moment could be suspended in time, it would be fine. I have everything.*

It was time for Babette to be introduced to Greta. Babette was having a conniption fit in the other room, whining pitifully and barking with insistence. After all, nobody locks Babette in another room. Everything is all about Babette. Just ask her. They braced themselves as they opened the study room/prison/nursery door.

Out she shot at a hundred miles per hour. She hadn't seen Kat much in a couple of days since she had been in the hospital, so when she found her, Babette was a wiggling, winking tornado. She flew onto the bed, halting abruptly; that is when she saw Greta.

You could practically read her mind. "What thing is this?" She sidled up to the sleeping infant and sniffed delicately. Then she lay motionless beside Kat and simply watched, cocking her head from side to side. Maybe ten minutes passed where Babette was absolutely still. Then Greta squawked in her sleep. Babette stood and sniffed gently at the infant again, but this time she sniffed the entire length of the sleeping baby. Kat was guarded because she couldn't absolutely predict Babette's reaction. Always affectionate and docile, Kat believed Babette would never hurt the baby. Yet Babette had always had the luxury of being the center of attention, a position of which she was quite fond, so how would she handle having to scoot over for a baby?

Babette continued to stare intently. As Greta fussed slightly, it seemed to dawn on Babette. "Why, she has brought me a puppy. It's a puppy." She positioned herself at Greta's feet. Greta kicked with her tiny foot and connected softly with Babette's nose. Babette, startled, assumed the play mode (front down on two paws and tail feathers high and wiggling in the back). Then her pink tongue appeared and gently licked Greta's tiny toes.

Never was there a mom as obsessive as Babette. Judging from her reaction, Babette must have secretly yearned for a little one all her life. She spent every waking moment watching over Greta. Kat had to keep an eye on Babette because she liked to nuzzle her face in Greta's neck—a practice frowned upon by both Greta and Kat. As that was not allowed, Babette would lie beside Greta, scooting over until every part of her body was touching against the infant.

Crying was not to be permitted. If Greta cried, whosoever was present must drop everything and attend to Greta's needs. Babette would see to it, and the demanding little dog would not be denied. She whimpered and pranced and barked if necessary, but you needed to hop to *now*. If someone had the audacity to take Greta to a well-baby appointment or something leaving the house empty, Babette would search from room to room, looking for her baby.

Greta slept in a padded dresser drawer in Kat and Bob's bedroom at night so she could be readily fed and reassured if she woke during the night. Babette, who had always slept in bed with Kat and Bob, now acted as sentry at the foot of the dresser. Babette would oversee Greta's feedings, diaper changes, and playtimes like she was the quality control expert of such matters. Sleep was at a premium. Greta awoke every two hours even on a good night. The couple felt as if they were walking underwater while they washed the mountain of clothes and sleepwalked through the night feedings. Even sleepless, the family recognized this as a golden time in their marriage and approached each day as a treasure.

Chapter VII

GRADUATION DAY

Graduation day was finally here. A hard-won civil engineering degree was the prize for two years of intense, unremitting study. Bob graduated magna cum laude, no mean feat in this academic arena.

Kat wanted to give Bob something really wonderful as a graduation gift. She, more than anyone, knew just how hard Bob worked and what they both had sacrificed for him to be successful. People suggested an expensive camera or watch to commemorate the occasion, but Kat had other ideas. She and Margaret put their heads together and masterminded a surprise for Bob. His parents and much-loved little sister Debbie were traveling from Pennsylvania to attend the ceremony. He was the first member of his family to graduate from college and was considered a fair-haired boy for this accomplishment, and they meant to see him walk that stage and accept his diploma.

Bob was told that it was Kat's mother who would be attending the ceremony and he was to pick her up at Phoenix Sky Harbor Airport from Flight 626 United Airlines at 8:00 AM. After he took off for the airport, Kat took Greta and Babette to Jennifer's, and Bob and Kat's house began buzzing with activity. A brunch was being staged for after the graduation ceremony that was complete with barbecued chicken, homemade potato salad, baked beans, coleslaw, and plenty of ice-cold beer.

Kat did not accompany Bob to the airport that day, but his family talked about the surprise for hours after arriving. Going to the airport, any airport is always grueling. There's the traffic and the parking to worry about, the deciding of which gate, and then the rat-racing through the airport mazes to arrive at the correct gate on time. Bob made it just under the wire.

At that time, Sky Harbor Airport was a small local airport—the type where the aircrafts taxied up to a one-story terminal building and the passengers descended stairs rolled up to the planes and walked across the tarmac to the terminal. In an era before airplane skyjacking and terrorists, you could actually meet someone at the arrival gate instead of waiting outside in the security area as we do today. Those waiting to meet passengers would stand behind a four-foot-high chain-link fence and watch the passengers disembark. Standing among the usual group of families, friends, and business acquaintances that gathered to meet arriving planes, Bob made small talk with the gentleman beside him. With the stairs in place and the door open on the airplane, Bob watched for Kat's mother to appear. While scanning the passengers, he noticed one bald-headed gentleman who bore a remarkable resemblance to his father, whom he hadn't seen in two years. The guy even walked like Bob's father with his lumbering gait. Bob commented to the gentleman with whom he had been chatting on the uncanny resemblance. In fact, a doppelganger! He stared in disbelief. Then he noticed that the woman beside the gentleman was a dead ringer for Margaret, his mother. It was. It was Margaret. Next to Margaret, Bob recognized his beautiful little sister Debbie. It dawned on Bob that his family had made the arduous, expensive plane trip to honor him by attending his graduation. No one was allowed on the landing strip, as the sign read, but that day, Bob skirted the barricade and ran the length to embrace his family. As he picked Debbie up off the ground and swung her in a circle, she said, "Congrats, Brudder," using a nickname she had called him since childhood. His mother kissed him on the cheek then brushed away the lipstick left behind with saliva-treated Kleenex, the privilege of mothers everywhere. Then he faced his father—a man whose approval he had sought since grade school. His father beamed, shaking his hand vigorously and saying, "Good job, son. You have made us proud." It justified every minute of those two dreadful years.

Chapter VIII

THE AIR FORCE LIFE FOR ME

Bob was dedicated to serving his country. It was how he was reared by a deeply patriotic father. He deemed it his honor and his duty to support and defend the Constitution and was proud to do so. Life in the armed forces though had some important differences to the civilian life. Some of the differences were nothing short of wonderful. Others differences were not so much.

There was an interesting demographic in the air force. People were mostly between the ages of eighteen to forty years, so no one was really old, and no one was really young. Career airmen generally retired at twenty years of service. That made the retirement age roughly around forty years old. This was plenty of time for a second career in civilian life with the ambition to work toward a second retirement while the armed-forces retirement check rolled in. Retirement at a young age was definitely seen as one of the advantages.

While illicit drug use is everywhere, it was seen minimally in the services and not to the extent seen in the civilian population as it was cause for immediate dishonorable discharge. Drug users didn't last long. Another difference is that everyone was fit and healthy. If not, they were honorably discharged. It was a sort of elitist environment.

Additionally, an individual joining the armed forces tended to have a certain personality profile. Maybe when the draft was instated, you might have found a more diverse population, but since the draft was abolished and enlistment was entirely voluntary, the person serving his country was necessarily of a certain character. This person lived life more by the book, adhered more to old-school values, and was more disciplined.

Further, that person enlisting in the service had to prove his worth by surviving boot camp, where many were eliminated who were, for instance, too immature to truly live up to the motto of "A few good men (women)."

After boot camp, the services practice an up-or-out policy. Every member was required to advance in the ranks according to a prescribed timetable or be separated from the service. While it may seem harsh, the policy assured excellence in the armed forces.

In our society, it seems that a percentage of our young men and women are ill prepared for life after they have graduated from high school. Suddenly, they are expected to act on an adult level with very little preparation. They may have passed algebra, but how does one land a job? If they are lucky enough to land a job, how does one keep it or advance within the organization? Other simple but crucial life skills that enhance success, such as how one balances a checkbook or stay on a budget, were never taught in the school system. These skills are easily as important as any philosophy class, and many of our young people, those people to whom we entrust the future of our country, are frighteningly inept and insecure.

They need to believe in themselves and need to feel they are part of something larger and more important, and for crying in the mud, they need the guidance of their elders. Attending boot camp was one critical step in their development because there they were shown principles for success. At the hands of some drill sergeant who was "Not your mother," one could learn how to commit and be a valuable member of a team, how to accept a challenge, and how to gain self-discipline and a sense of self-respect. Forging these new recruits from lost teenagers into fine young airmen benefitted the entire country in a long-range, inestimable way.

With boot camp out of the way, there was a battery of tests administered to each new recruit to determine aptitude. This was a good practice as it often led to developing a trade. The recruit would use this jumping-off point to establish a lifelong vocation. Perhaps the aptitude test reflected a propensity for criminal law? The recruit would be assigned to the air police division and go on to become a peace officer of the law in civilian life once discharged. They might show an interest and aptitude for medicine guiding them to become a medic in the services and afterward catapulting them forward in the medical field in some capacity after completing their tour of duty. This again was a benefit not just to the young person but to society as a whole as this could be the step that prevented an individual from pursuing unacceptable lifestyles, like joining a gang or using illegal means to fund a living.

Another benefit was the GI bill that made the American dream accomplishable. This was a leg up to pursue an education at the college level, fueling the United States with motivated, educated, professionally minded individuals. It provided a foundation not just as a boost to the economy but also by the impartation of the necessary education for a viable democratic society.

Once the young person completed an education, he or she could count on a VA loan to assist them to purchase a home. Owning a home has always been such a significant accomplishment. It created a sense of ownership, devotion to community, and dedication to preserving a way of life. The prosperity of America was profoundly affected at the grass roots thanks to these benefits.

There was the lure of travel, of course. Bob and Kat had already been to Italy, Arizona, Washington State, and Pennsylvania and would soon be relocated to Fairfield, California. Bob had also been to Mississippi for his basic training and Texas for officer candidate school. With the goal of serving twenty years, they expected to see even more of the country with each new reassignment. They enjoyed travel and were young and adventurous.

The benefits notwithstanding, there were lots of hurdles for a family trying to make their way in the armed services. There's the old song that goes like this: "You'll never get rich a diggin' a ditch," which couldn't be truer. The personnel were meagerly paid. There might even be a method to this madness in some cases as the very young airmen stayed in a dormitory-style situation called a barracks, giving them stability to grow in. But if you're a young family trying to eke out a living, its franks and beans every night because regardless of the rank or the performance on the job, the wages were poorly reimbursed compared to the civilian pay scale. No unions intervening here.

Now here's a disadvantage for you. These assets are incredibly attractive in a peacetime situation, but what if at any time there is a war declared? The risk/benefit ratio is turned on its ear then. A question that all must ask themselves or refrain from volunteering is "Am I willing to lay down my life for my country and the Constitution?" For Bob, there was no hesitation; in fact, that was what he signed up to do, but it's not for everybody.

The travel was a nicety that added spice to life. However, included in the possibility of travel was an assignment known by the unlucky as a remote. If the truth be told, the air force tended to spread this misery around to most of their unsuspecting youth. These assignments meant relocation to hideous, unlivable areas that were "unaccompanied" (meaning that the family was left behind to flounder), and it was often for a year at a time. The servicemen could find themselves stationed at Kotzebue, Alaska, in an icy wasteland with sixty-degree-below-zero temperatures and no sun for nine months and looking at a year's separation from their families.

Remote or no, the family unit is frequently a casualty of the armed-services lifestyle. The poor pay and the constant relocation, invariably every three years, took its toll on the very fiber of the marriage. A move to a new house meant many financial hardships that ate up resources. These hardships were not immediately apparent at first glance. Imagine the cost of a cleaning deposit, a pet deposit, and first and last months' rent that a family had to scrape together every three years. That cleaning-deposit refund, that's a scam. No matter how clean a young couple left a rental, the landlords would drum up a reason to retain the majority of the deposit, with the renters powerless to get the sorely needed refund. That stolen money was necessary for the deposits on the next rental. Other things like new curtains were an expense with every move because the old ones never fit. And of course, a struggling air force family wasn't realistically a candidate to buy a house with the hope of getting some appreciation back—not with another move just around the corner. Essentially, it was the cost of starting from scratch visited upon them every three years.

Even if the there was not a remote, there were frequently new trainings scheduled or something called TDY, or temporary duty, that separated a family. The wretched loneliness threatened even the solidest marriages. A run-of-the-mill move meant a family was cut off from the support system of their extended family and friends and was tasked with making fresh alliances in a new location at the drop of a hat. Not so easy to do always when one was a stranger in a strange land, some of the places right here in the United States being pretty strange. Infidelity and divorce were rampant, and only the bravest, most devoted marriages sustained.

The psychological impact of leaving the familiar and relocating caused a gnawing sense of disorientation. Navigating a new city and learning the layout of the streets and freeways was bewildering. Where was the elementary school? Where was the post office? How far away was the library? Was there a nursing school in the area? How about if they wanted to go out for dinner? Where was the closest restaurant, and was it any good or way too expensive? Familiarity establishes a sense of belonging and contributes to the quality of life. It can be depressing to have to start over every three years.

Soon Kat and Bob developed a system to overcome this disorientation in record time. They had a list of necessary services, including gas stations, libraries, dry cleaners, schools, restaurants, post offices, mall locations, hardware stores, and grocery stores. They would split these services in half, would locate the best and closest selection for the service indicated and after completing the task, would meet at the local grocery store to share information.

When they relocated to Fairfield and after the household goods had been delivered, they each took their list and embarked on their respective goals armed with the local telephone book as a guide. Bob took the big old white Chevy truck, and Kat took her classic Mustang convertible, and off they went. They were fortunate to have already found a SuperMart grocery store on a corner and agreed to meet there when finished.

Kat completed her list and arrived first at the SuperMart and, since Bob was still not there, decided to do the shopping for the week. She carefully selected each item with regard for their budget. As she checked out, she watched for Bob, but he must have still been following the yellow brick road because he was nowhere to be found. She loaded the Mustang slowly while monitoring the parking lot for the Chevy truck, but still no Bob. There were perishables in the groceries, ice cream and expensive items like meat. She would run the groceries home since it was only two blocks away, unload, put away the perishables, and then return to wait for Bob.

She started the engine, turned on to the main road, and pulled the Mustang over into one of two left-hand turning lanes. Out of the corner of her eye, she glimpsed the tall white Chevy truck pull up next to her. Bob had caught up to her! She was in a playful mood. She took her shirt by the hem, pulled it up over her face, rose up in the seat, and turned toward Bob, affording him a full monty view of her bare chest. She dropped her shirt back down laughing and looked over at the truck to see Bob's face.

Staring back at her was not the amused face of her husband but that of a very old and withered-looking oriental man. He had a look of sheer horror on his pale face, with his eyes as round as silver dollars and his mouth forming a perfect O. Kat could hear him utter something in a language she didn't comprehend. Then he floored his truck though the light was still red and turned left sharply, leaving rubber tracks as he peeled out.

Kat was mortified as she told Bob what had happened. He, though, thought it was great fun and laughed until tears ran down his face. When Bob repeated this story, and he did with great relish to anyone who would listen (even though Kat advised against it), he would refer to the story as the day Kat almost killed a man with her chest.

Chapter IX

NURSE HATEFUL

After graduation, Bob was assigned to Travis Air Force Base in Fairfield, California—his first position as a professional civil engineer. Kat was delighted with the assignment for two reasons: First, even though Fairfield was more northern than Los Angeles, California, it was basically still a place of comfort for her. She was a rare, actual native—having been born in Corona, California, as was her mother—and considered California as her personal playground. She had been to Disneyland every year of her life. Regardless of where the family was stationed, they returned home to California yearly to vacation with their extended family. A trip to Disneyland was always one of the highlights. Kat knew all the rides, every concession stand, and where every bathroom was. The Pacific Ocean ran in her blood from spending countless contented hours at Newport or Huntington Beach. It didn't hurt matters that her extended family lived south in Riverside, California, which was just a five-hour trip by car over the Grapevine. She was home.

The second reason that Kat was delighted with the location of the assignment was that she could attend nursing school at Solano Community College to finish up her nursing degree and start her clinical rotations. She had attended one nursing program after another every time the air force relocated the family. Each school was picky about accepting the credits from another institution, making it

disappointingly necessary to repeat courses to matriculate to the next
level. Kat believed privately that this was a bottom-line issue so the
school could ensure a student base for each level of the curriculum,
but she couldn't prove anything, and in the end, it was what it was. So
she chose to take it on the chin, played their silly game, and repeated
whatever she needed to qualify and was thereby accepted into the
program.

She would soon be able to don an official nursing uniform. She
couldn't wait to go shopping for scrubs. What fun! In days gone by,
nursing uniforms had to be white and preferably shapeless and ugly.
The uniform was once accompanied by a nursing cap known as a crown
that was awarded ceremonially to those brave souls who graduated from
nursing school after surviving the rigorous training. Those uniforms
had been replaced now by brightly decorated, cute scrubs consisting of
a stylish top with matching pants. Kat was proud to wear the uniform
that designated her as a nurse and announced to the world that she
achieved her lifelong goal.

Nursing school referred to the book-learning portion of the
program as didactics. For Kat, that was the easy part. It wasn't that she
was off-the-chart smarter than the next person at all. It was just that
her aptitude was well suited to those requisite courses. She enjoyed
chemistry—even organic chemistry. She could even go so far as to say
it made sense to her. She loved the challenge and the learning, the
discovery that tied anatomy and physiology to biochemistry and made
it all logical and beautifully ordered. She adored the applied physics
that was central to everything—even something as simple as the
working of an intravenous feeding. Because of her diligent study of the
fundamentals of medicine, she *understood* pharmacology on a chemical
level. She loved, loved, loved school and ate up the scientific part. The
party was over now though. She was starting clinical rotations.

The student nurses were assigned to a rotation in each of the
medical disciplines to develop hospital-nursing skills and practically
apply the knowledge they had been given. It was that whole "saving
someone's life in the trenches" that had her worried. Her level of
expertise or lack thereof could make the difference between life
and death for a patient. She had been in the program long enough
to know that if a patient was going bad that it could happen quickly
and it was the nurse who cared for the patient, who was familiar and
knowledgeable about the patient, who saved the day. If a patient had
undergone surgery then developed early warning signs like a fever or
a reduced urine output, the nurse *had* to know her medicine and be
vigilant because these symptoms could be subtle and still telegraph

acute problems. Kat wanted to be not just a good but a great nurse worthy of her patients' trust.

She bolstered her courage and readied herself to put her broad range of medical knowledge to use. Kat's first rotation in hospital nursing was to be on the "med/surg" floor, or medical/surgical floor, where she would encounter many different types of patients and medical conditions. She was assigned Nurse Hathaway as her clinical instructor, known to the nursing students enrolled in the program as Nurse Hateful because she was hard as Chinese algebra and took her teaching responsibility as seriously as a wartime drill sergeant. You were going to get a good education, no question, but you weren't going to enjoy it.

On the first day of rotation, Nurse Hathaway appeared clad in the traditional white nursing garb with support stockings and orthopedic-looking white shoes and sporting the foregone white crown cap. That should have been a dead giveaway to her students that they were in for a spanking.

Nurse Hathaway assigned each nurse a patient load and watched them like a hawk. She carefully evaluated her nursing students and assessed their particular educational needs, diligently sniffing out weaknesses. Kat's first-ever patient was a noncompliant nineteen-year-old type 1 diabetic named Donovan, who had been brought into the emergency room in a diabetic coma. He had long, oily brown hair and a torso covered with tattooed skulls and four-lettered words. His medical history was full of drug use, alcoholism, and a blatant refusal to comply with his diabetic regime. This was his fourth visit to the ER, according to his medical chart, for very similar medical circumstances. He had no family, no friends, no insurance, and no regard for his diabetic-care regime. This was the third day of the coma, and he had yet to regain consciousness in spite of every medical intervention—a red flag for a bad prognosis.

His case went to the medical ethics committee to determine his treatment plan as there was no one to speak for him and he was not conscious. Their decision, based on his troubling labs and flat EEG (an EEG reflects the level of brain activity, his indicating minimal brain activity), was to discontinue life support and label the patient with Do Not Resuscitate. "Do not resuscitate," otherwise known as DNR, is a legal mandate not to provide CPR or advanced cardiac life support if a person were to stop breathing or their heart were to stop beating.

This was really tough for Kat. That night, she thought about the decision, mulled over how she felt about it, and discovered she was outraged. She railed to Bob about it self-righteously. "Nobody should be put on a 'Do not resuscitate' order. Everyone admitted to that hospital should have every chance to recover. How dare they accept a patient's trust then sentence them to die? Do they think they're God or Dr. Kevorkian or something?"

The committee had scheduled Thursday at 3:00 PM to remove Donovan from life support, and Kat attended, holding his hand and talking calmly to him. The day wore on, and Donovan persevered, breathing on his own. Nurse Hathaway assured her that was not unusual; it sometimes takes a couple of hours or even a couple of days for a compromised patient to succumb.

That was a bad night for Kat. She cried and vented to Bob, who quietly listened, nodding his head in concurrence when it seemed she wanted support. The next morning, Kat received her assignments during nursing report and was told that not only had Donovan survived the night but, in fact, was conscious. She ran to his room to find him sipping water and changing the TV channel obsessively.

"Hi, Donovan. My name is Kat," she said. "I am the nurse assigned to your care."

He looked her up and down suggestively and said, "Hey, baby, when's my sponge bath?"

Before the day was up, he regained the strength to make a pass at her and even felt well enough to pinch her on the bottom.

The experience reinforced Kat's position on the "Do not resuscitate" question. The student nurses were required to write a daily chronicle of their experiences in a journal that Nurse Hathaway always reviewed. Kat wrote in scathing detail about her animosity for "Do not resuscitate" directives, and Nurse Hathaway saw her duty.

From that day on, Kat was assigned only "Do not resuscitate" patients. From each patient, Kat gleaned new insight concerning the "Do not resuscitate" directive that challenged her position. One patient, though, enlightened Kat to the point that she had to rethink her stand.

Marisol Guadalupe Garcia Hernandez was originally from Castile, Spain. Her complexion was so pale that it was almost transparent and her waist-length hair as black as a winter-storm cloud. She was a brilliant attorney with a prestigious law practice who had proven herself in the courts as a seasoned professional. One afternoon, she developed a headache that no aspirin could accommodate. Afterward, she began to forget things. She could conveniently explain it all away until the day in court when she lost her train of thought, not something Marisol had ever done, and then lost her vision.

A trip to her physician and a CAT scan diagnosed a malignant brain tumor known as a sarcoma. The news was grim because it had metastasized, or spread, to many of her other body organs. No medical intervention could fix that. According to the physician, Marisol had maybe three weeks to live, and because of the location and size of the tumor, it was, for all practical purposes, inoperable.

Her large, devoted family was devastated and plagued the physician to do *something* to save this lovely, intelligent woman who was such a force in the world. They talked to the physician of surgical procedures to excise the cancer that enabled the family to climb on board the good ship of hope. The surgeon explained that removing the cancer from the brain might, at best, buy a bit of time but would undeniably cause Marisol extended and useless suffering. The family insisted that even minutes were precious to them and maybe, just maybe, Marisol would be that miracle that everyone has heard about.

By the time that Marisol was assigned to Kat as a patient, she had endured four surgeries to remove the spreading cancer from her brain. She was paralyzed, nonresponsive, and ventilator dependent. As Kat bathed Marisol, she was saddened to note that there were tears streaming down Marisol's porcelain cheeks, and she knew in her heart that Marisol was in there, hated the lack of dignity and purpose, and was a prisoner of her family's great esteem.

Kat went home a changed woman. She thought piteously of Marisol's predicament, of the telltale tears trailing down her face, and of the painful and pointless future she would endure and realized the importance of a patient going on record to establish a directive to release a family from the burden of making this emotional decision. No less important is that of a hospital's sacred, irrefutable contract to abide by that on-record decision of a patient. Kat went on to complete her nursing program and, in fact, graduated as the top graduate, but that day, she realized that ideals were a luxury reserved for those residing in an ivory tower—those not haunted by Marisol's tears and who did not witness the agonized family unable to sentence to death a cherished mother. She learned that virtue is indeed not virtuous if untested by fire and what it meant to be a true patient advocate. That day, she became the good nurse she wished to be. Compliments of Nurse Hateful.

Chapter X

PAWS FOR LIFE

As part of the nursing curriculum, each student nurse was tasked to develop a nursing project. The project would be central to her graduating thesis. There was a lot of latitude where this project was concerned, but basically, it had to be important, spectacular, innovative, imaginative, community based, and relevant. An example of a project that qualified in the past was a food bank to feed the hungry established by one of the graduating nursing classes two years before that withstood time and became a relied-upon community resource.

Kat thought about what interested her, drawing upon experiences that made her uniquely an individual and contemplating where her passion lay. She looked around at the demographics and the services available in the immediate area. There were no medical-response dog groups, therapy dogs, or service dog facilities. She felt very strongly that the relationship between animals and humans has a profoundly therapeutic effect. Evidence suggests that animal-assisted therapy can improve blood pressure readings, ameliorate stress, and assist a patient toward physical and emotional health. A large-scale operation was beyond her capabilities, but if she got a toehold in the community proving the concept's worth and making the services known to the public at large, it would be valued enough to blossom into something much more substantial.

Kat investigated the requirements, noting that medical-response dogs were highly trained and had extremely stringent requirements. Service dog requirements were much more lax but still enormously time-consuming. The least restrictive was the role of therapy dog. In fact, the only requirements for training a therapy dog were that they be under the guidance of a certified trainer; be current with their vaccinations; and be friendly, predictable, nonaggressive, and obedient. Those dogs deemed characteristically acceptable were then trained and certified by the American Kennel Association to help people dealing with medical, physical, emotional, cognitive, or social disabilities to progress to wellness.

Kat submitted her proposal for a plan that she called Paws for Life to Nurse Hathaway. She came armed with enthusiasm, touting research and statistics to support the credibility of the idea. Nurse Hathaway found the proposal refreshing and cutting-edge and was overwhelmingly in favor of the idea.

The first objective was to achieve certification for Kat as a trainer, and then it was to achieve the same for her dog, Babette, as a therapy dog. She identified a training site in Sacramento for certification, but designating a venue for Babette to demonstrate her gift of positive human-dog interaction had Kat plenty worried. Fortunately, Nurse Hathaway had a friend in a pediatric skilled-nursing facility called Shady Pines that she felt would be amenable to Babette conducting therapy visits. Kat's long-range goal was to act as a spearhead to carve a place in the medical profession within her community for the legitimate therapeutic use of animals in healing. The plan was put in progress.

The certification piece actually turned out to be a pleasure for both owner and dog though they had to commute an hour and a half to Sacramento. Much of the fundamentals of the program were really just flashbacks from obedience school. The dog must be prepared to demonstrate the basics: "Sit," "Come," "Stand," and "Stay," but all must be achieved with a loose leash. Straining on the leash reflected a lack of control on the trainer's part, which is unacceptable in a medical facility and around frail patients. Exposure was key to acclimating the animal. Babette was to be in the presence of many different people, other dogs, varied experiences, and various medical equipments and medical conditions. This is a critical element of the training. In order for the dog to be truly therapeutic, the animal must be comfortable and not view these settings as threatening. Additionally, Babette picked up some "breaking the ice" tricks that Kat thought would appeal to the pediatric population with whom she'd be working. Babette could rise onto her short back legs and pirouette in a circle while waving her arms. This was adorable and a feat she was gloriously proud to perform. She could shake hands, though she felt obligated to issue a kiss as long as she was at it, so that trick was still a work in progress. She could lie on the floor and cover her eyes with both paws, for whatever that was worth. Kat called it as saying a prayer, and it proved to be a hit later.

Kat and Babette then joined a therapy group in Sacramento designed to band together for the cause of promoting animal-human therapy. It was seven caring, energetic women with an abiding love for animals and a belief that all beings on earth are intricately and eternally interrelated. Monica was the informal leader of the group. She had a Yorkie named Diva, otherwise known as a purse pet because it was small enough to fit nicely into Monica's handbag and accompanied her everywhere—even to the grocery store, courtesy of its therapy dog vest. Diva had a bit of an attitude, believing that the world revolved around her exclusively, and if you had asked Monica, she would have had to confirm that was the case.

All those people who suggest that pets and their owners look alike would be vindicated if they saw Monica and Diva side by side. Both were tiny, looking Lilliputian in a world of giants. Diva had the traditional silky brown, black, and tan coat of Yorkies and seemed fearlessly oblivious of her size. She would charge in where dogs of far greater size would have hesitated to tread and would challenge any dog daring to act uppity to a good butt-whipping. Monica herself looked remarkably similar to her dog in the face with her turned-up nose and the same bright, soulful brown eyes. Both sported identical top notches gathered at the crowns of their heads that were tied with usually pink bows.

Another member of the group, who was named Megan, owned a slinky black-and-white tuxedo cat she called Oreo that she was convinced was destined to live its life usefully as a therapy animal. She and Oreo had been with the therapy group for seven months, trying to qualify for that all-important therapy vest and emblem so Oreo could spread his particular charm to heal and uplift the suffering. Megan would call out commands like "Sit," and Oreo would contemptuously ignore her, preferring to clean a body part instead. He also had an unfortunate habit of biting people, so between the disregard for the commands and the propensity to bite, it had been a challenge thus far. When approached by one of the qualifying committee while standing for certification, Oreo had a tendency to arch his back and cock his ears down and to the side, hopping and hissing angrily with cougar-like ferocity—all behaviors frowned upon by the certifying examiners. To the support group's credit, however, they were nothing if not patient, and Never Say Die was their motto. So they continued to train Megan and Oreo with the goal of certification in mind, and everyone in the support committee was pulling for them.

That was one goal of the therapy-support group: to generate new members by familiarizing them with the paces that would be expected of the animals by the American Kennel's Canine Good Citizen Certification and would be expected of the handlers by the American Humane Society. Babette and Kat had the benefit of the support group's tutelage, and thanks to their wonderful coaching, Kat and Babette were each successfully certified.

Babette victoriously received her therapy dog vest with the qualifying patch. Generally speaking, Babette was not a big fan of wearing clothes of any type—even a collar was suspect. But for a while, she had modeled doll clothes and diapers and managed to survive the humiliating experience. So she condescendingly donned the vest though with a long-suffering expression on her face. She would have put on that vest and a doll's whole wardrobe if she had known what was to come eventually.

Shady Pines was a pediatric, long-term, continuous skilled-nursing facility for children who were developmentally disabled, needed post hospitalization skilled nursing, respite care, or had complex medical needs. It was located on an acre of wooded land that was landscaped and maintained by the community at large on a volunteer basis, and it was breathtaking. People had donated their time, their money, their flowers and all the existing playground equipment. Their hearts answered the needs of these sick, innocent children, and they felt honored to do so.

The clinical facility itself was managed by a registered nurse called Mama Evelyn by all. She guarded the welfare of the facility and its denizens like a lioness. The nurses that Mama Evelyn afforded the privilege to practice there at Shady Pines were so caring and competent that *angel* was not too lofty a term to describe their role. To walk into the ward was nothing less than a spiritual experience, the love and dedication of the staff almost palpable.

The population at Shady Pines was children ranging from infancy to eighteen years of age who had debilitating medical illnesses. The numbers fluctuated because the patients would either recover and be discharged or sometimes a much-sadder outcome would occur and leave a vacancy. The day that Kat and Babette were scheduled to do their first therapy session there were twelve children in residence.

Kat and Babette arrived at Shady Pines through an ivy-covered gated entrance and parked in the front. Babette was outfitted in her newly earned green vest. You could read the disgust on her face, but once the vest was strapped on, what was a dog to do? They left the car and walked up to the entrance of the facility. Kat delivered a lengthy lecture to Babette reminding her that she must comply with commands with a "loose leash" so she mustn't strain, all more directed at her own nervousness than anything that benefitted Babette. When they walked through the door, Babette dropped her tail and looked strangely at Kat, as if imploring her, "What can you be thinking?" Kat knelt on one knee, trying to reassure the little dog, but the expression on Babette's face was one of terror and confusion. Kat pulled on the leash to lead Babette forward, but she dug in her heels and refused to cooperate. There were no two ways about it; Babette was scared. Kat didn't know what to do. She waited to give Babette time to adjust, but after thirty minutes, Kat had to concede failure and disappointment and opened the door to leave. Babette bolted to the car like she was shot from cannon, jumped in the front seat and sat trembling. Kat sat beside her, gathered Babette in her arms, and wondered wildly what was going through Babette's mind. What suffering had been communicated to her to cause her to react so adversely? Kat knew Babette to be empathetic at the very least; maybe the burden was too great? It hadn't occurred to Kat this would be hard for Babette. Babette crawled into Kat's lap, seeking reassurance, and stubbornly could not be persuaded to get down.

At last, Kat was about to decide to throw in the towel when an odd thing happened. Babette licked Kat on the cheek, climbed off her lap, jumped back out of the car through the driver's door, and walked over to the entrance, tail still at half-mast. Kat scrambled to open the door to the facility, and Babette went willingly to the nursing station, still trembling slightly. As they waited, you could have sensed Babette's courageous struggle. Kat thought to herself that if Babette could talk, you might have heard her determinably saying to herself, "Oh yeah, it's on."

Children could be heard giggling, crying, arguing, and playing throughout the clinic. All the sounds you'd expect of a pediatric facility echoed through the halls. Kat was pleased to see Babette stick to her training by remaining stock-still, undeterred by the din. The nurses were overwhelmingly taken with Babette. They each introduced themselves to her and offered to pet her, but Kat explained that Babette was still in training. The truth was that after Babette freaked out, Kat didn't want to push her luck.

Mama Evelyn was there taking it all in, wise as a sage. She spoke to Babette in a calm tone with reverence in her voice, helping her to calm down. She told Kat that she was going to monitor all initial interactions, protective as always of her patients. "Let's start easy," she said. "We'll go visit Ms. Louwelsa."

Louwelsa was a ten-year-old girl who had been diagnosed with that flesh-eating disease in her left thigh at Christmas and spent two months in the hospital. The prognosis had been poor, having only a 12 percent chance to live and with even greater odds that if she did survive, she would almost certainly lose her leg. Yet against these depressing odds, she lived to tell the harrowing story. By some miracle, she did not suffer the amputation but still required a good deal of nursing assistance, physical therapy, and rehabilitation, so she had been at the facility for three weeks. She was charming with a sunny disposition, almost as if every single minute was a gift for which she was grateful. When she met a new person, she would introduce herself with a lopsided curtsy, of all things, and say, "How do you do? I'm Lou-Lou."

Babette walked into Lou-Lou's room very reservedly—none of the usual prancing, jumping, and licking. She was on her very best therapy dog behavior. Lou-Lou, however, acted like Christmas had come early. She limped as fast as a little girl with one healing leg could limp, nightgown flying, and descended upon Babette. She held Babette, chatting gaily, rubbing her ears, and kissing her on her little wet nose. And Babette? Well, she was overjoyed. Oddly, she didn't wiggle or become hyper, but the evident joy on her face could be felt across the room like electricity. She was in her element. Mama Evelyn appeared to be satisfied that Babette could behave appropriately. She had to actually pry Babette out of Lou-Lou's arms with Lou-Lou protesting loudly the whole while. "I want Babette to sleep with me," she wailed. Mama Evelyn told Lou-Lou that Babette was a working dog and was here to visit with all the children, but it was still a battle to get Babette free.

Mama Evelyn thought for a second. She mentally reviewed the patient population for the next interactions. She regarded Babette slyly then said, "This one's tough, old girl. If you can help this little cherub, then you've got my vote." So it was to be a test. Kat held her breath and said a silent prayer for Babbette.

The three walked down a rather-dark corridor and turned a corner. The pitiful weeping of an inconsolable child resounded in the hall the whole trip. Crying was a real problem for Babette—not one she could be trained to ignore. She was always one to want to fix whatever might be troubling the child *now*. So when she heard crying, it tended to be a trigger causing her to become desperate and hyperactive. *Stand firm,* Kat pleaded in her mind.

Upon entering the room, the source of the incessant crying was seen. There on the floor in an open playpen lay Dillon whimpering.

Dillon was a two-year-old boy born with Downs syndrome. Individuals born with Down syndrome suffer from a misplaced chromosome, just how misplaced the chromosome determining the severity of the syndrome. Some were minimally affected, had borderline IQs, worked productively, and lived long and satisfying lives.

Then there were those having the worst physical and medical ramifications of the chromosomal abnormality. This was Dillon's lot. His ears were located very low on his head, giving him an odd look. His mouth too was unusual with his lips turned perpetually downward and his tongue protruding at all times. Other things made the syndrome immediately apparent even if one was not familiar with the cause. There was a very unconventional look to his face because the bridge of his nose was oddly flat, making his eyes appear even more widely spaced than they actually were. Additionally, there were physical differences, such as his fingers that were abnormally short. The physical idiosyncrasies that were visible, however, were not those things that caused him to be debilitated; it was those things that weren't readily apparent. He had a congenital heart condition, not unusual for a Downs baby. He was mentally retarded, also an expected find for a child with Downs; however, there was a spectrum that ran from an IQ as high as seventy points downward. The physician believed Dillon's IQ to be at best around thirty, putting him in the profoundly retarded category. Also, he was born deaf, making any interaction difficult.

Dillon spent much of the time crying, with sleep being his only reprieve, though the nurses had tried everything. They took turns holding him, walking him, and reading to him. The cause for the crying could only be surmised. It did not seem to be pain related in any way. It did not respond to any pain medications. It might even have been his approach to communication. No one knew for certain.

Kat and Babette stood in the doorway, gazing at Dillon with Babette looking stricken. They walked together up to the unenclosed playpen. (Dillon was not ambulatory, so it could be safely left open.) First, Babette lay very still in Dillon's view. Dillon noticed her but did not respond other than to make eye contact. Babette inched closer to the toddler very slowly, making no sudden movements. Dillon continued crying, but you could tell by him focusing his eyes that he was starting to engage with Babette. Babette inched a bit closer, and Dillon reached out to her. Then he stopped crying and just stared at her, hiccupping. Babette did not move. Not for twenty minutes. The two lay motionless, eyeing each other the entire time. Dillon continued to be placated, and eventually, his eyelids grew heavy, and he slid off to sleep with his index finger still touching Babette's right paw.

They cleared the room, leaving a sleeping Dillon, and Mama Evelyn stared at Babette with newfound respect. "Now I'm impressed," she told Babette, who rewarded Mama Evelyn with a broad dog smile and a wag of her fluffy tail.

The rest of the afternoon Babette spent waddling around the ward with the children enthralled. She set up therapy counseling in the community-recreation room, where the TV resided, and she worked the room like a seasoned politician. She performed a couple of her ice-breaking tricks to thundering cheers. She rose up on her short legs and pirouetted like a ballerina, giving the children a wave as she completed her circle. She said her prayers, delighting the little guys who joined in to give their own prayer of thanks to God for Babette. She laid a fluffy head on a little boy's lap and gazed at him with her warm brown eyes with unrestrained affection, basking in the delight of the child. She snuck in some of those puppy kisses that were taboo; they were going to have to work on that. She was a hit. There was a good deal of speculation among the ranks over just whose turn it was to hold and talk to Babette next, resulting in a couple of bitter altercations. Mama Evelyn had to intervene and hand out consecutive numbers and restrict time sessions to ten minutes apiece. Babette was having the best time of her life. She was conducting herself professionally like a good therapy dog except for the occasional slobbery kiss administered in a weak moment although she knew better, and she managed a guilty look whenever Kat caught her. Babette loved kids, and these kids radiated the need to be loved. This was what she lived for!

It came time for their two o'clock nap, so the children bid Babette good-bye, and Kat proceeded to ready herself and Babette to leave.

Suddenly, Babette turned and began tugging at the leash and walking insistently down a corridor not formerly explored. This was a no-no because the handler had to demonstrate control at all times. Kat tugged surreptitiously on the leash, not wanting Mama Evelyn to pick up on the disobedience. They had done so well, and Kat was counting on a favorable evaluation. Their success and the success of the plan to establish a therapy-training center here in Fairfield depended on a good evaluation from Mama Evelyn. The alternative was to follow Babette's lead, acting as if that had been the plan the whole time. But the truth was, Babette was calling the shots.

Babette insistently led Kat down a hallway to a room occupied by two bedbound children. Kat noted that Babette was trembling again and surmised that whatever had bothered Babette earlier would be found in this room.

It was immediately obvious why Babette's presence had not been summoned earlier by Mama Evelyn to this room. This room represented truly respite care. These children were located to this facility not with the hope of recovery or even medical care but to spell the parents. This provision of care alleviated the parents of the crushing demand of attending to the overpowering needs of these children, almost like a day care, giving the parents some temporary relief. It was also designed to provide a positive experience for the child. Everyone needs to be in the company of their peers regardless. To be in the company of other children is a luxury they might not have otherwise enjoyed.

Both children were girls in their early teens. They were encumbered by tubes and monitors recording their respiration rates, blood pressure rates, and pulse rates. Essentially, these girls were nonresponsive. The first girl, Ellen, had been in a coma for four years. Babette went to this bed, nosing the girl's hand that draped over the side. She seemed immediately uninterested and did not hesitate but turned and left Ellen's bed side.

The other girl, Leslie, was a drowning victim. She had fallen and broken through the ice of a mountain stream and was enveloped helplessly by the current and submerged in the icy water for not less than twenty minutes. There were success stories of victims surviving when submerged in freezing temperatures, but under most circumstances, being deprived for twenty minutes of oxygen had dire neurological consequences. There was no strict algorithm of what to expect. The brain injury that resulted was a consequence of what area of the brain was afflicted. Many times the victim was left functionally blind, deaf, and speechless, depending on the extent of the injury to the brain. From what Kat could tell, Leslie was not animated in any way.

Babette stood up on her short legs, bracing herself on the edge of the low cot and laying her head on Leslie's chest. Kat saw no response and tried to encourage Babette to vacate the room, but Babette was having none of it. She could be stubborn when it called for it. Kat sat in an available chair by the bed and resigned herself to see this through on Babette's time. "OK, girl," she said. "You've done an outstanding job today. We'll do it your way."

Ten minutes passed then twenty. Kat let her mind wander while Babette nudged Leslie gently and patted her with her paw, alternating between sitting and standing by the cot. Just as Kat was daydreaming about what to make for dinner, she heard the strains of a sweet voice resonate through the room. Kat bolted upright in shock and looked around to discover the source. What she saw was so astonishing that she would never be quite the same afterward. Those scientific truths that had dictated her world in the past were now subject to question. There was Leslie—lying in the same precise, unchanged position—motionless except for the movement of her lips. She was singing "Amazing Grace" with a melodious, creaky voice in perfect pitch:

"Amazing grace, how sweet the sound, that saved a wretch like me. I once was lost but now am found was blind but now I see."

Kat tried to stand up, but her legs failed her, and she sat back down in the chair with a thump. She looked at Babette, who seemed satisfied and had vacated the side of Leslie's bed and was ready to leave. Kat looked to the doorway and saw Mama Evelyn standing on the threshold with a shocked look of disbelief on her pale face. She gripped the doorframe like it was a lifeline holding her erect. For a worried moment, Kat feared that Mama Evelyn was going to faint. In fact, she wasn't completely sure that she wasn't going to lose consciousness as well. When the refrain ended, the room's silence was like a physical blow.

Kat, Babette, and Mama Evelyn left the room together in stunned silence. As they walked toward the exit, Kat tried to stage a getaway. She had no words for what had just transpired and found the whole thing unsettling. As always, Mama Evelyn read her like a novel and insisted she stop and drink a cup of tea before going so they could review the day. After the two had fixed their tea, Mama Evelyn situated the three of them on the couch with Babette in the middle. "Well, how do you think it went, Kat?" Mama Evelyn inquired.

Kat was mute, still in shock and could say nothing.

"Look," Mama Evelyn said. "I know that was pretty eerie back there, but I have seen another example of this happening. I had one drowning victim three years ago named Billy, who had a whole repertoire of songs: 'Jingle Bells,' 'Frosty the Snowman,' and the 'Itsy Bitsy Spider.' Those were the only things the child could utter. He too was unresponsive, thought to be blind, mute, and deaf, and could not communicate in any other way. When the drowning incident occurred, it spared at least that part of the brain that permits singing. You've heard of people who stuttered so badly that talking in a conversation was impossible yet they could sing perfectly well?"

Kat mulled that over and agreed that she had seen a couple of singers who stuttered badly but sang beautifully. She looked Mama Evelyn in the eye and asked pointedly, "Has Leslie ever done that before?"

"No," Mama Evelyn admitted. "But maybe that's because no one but Babette ever gave her the chance."

Kat was skeptical about the explanation but clung to it just the same because if not that, then what? The two women discussed the day, and for the most part, Mama Evelyn was favorably impressed with Babette. She even tried to get Kat to donate the dog to Shady Pines, maintaining that the children needed her and Babette was born to stay with them. There was some discussion about how sanitary doggy kisses might or might not be and to work on that one element because of infection control. The two women came to a consensus about establishing Saturdays as therapy-session days for Babette, and then Kat picked up an exhausted Babette and made for the car. She had a lot to think about.

Chapter XI

SHAKE, RATTLE, AND ROLL

They bought their first home in a small middle-class neighborhood in Fairfield close to Travis Air Base, with the Mount Washington Elementary School located at the end of the block. The three bedrooms, two-baths detached home even had a garage and seemed like a palace to the couple. The front yard had dish-sized pink roses growing in a planter adorning the front yard and a well-established, good-sized willow tree with beautiful, drooping branches that danced in the wind. The backyard was small, containing only a semi aboveground pool surrounded by decking and a natural-gas barbecue. The neighbors were friendly, and the tree-lined street teemed with children to play with Greta. They began their life with hope for a bright future.

The first thing they did after moving into their home was to fence the front yard with a five-foot-high chain-link fence and put a doggy door in the front door. The pool in the backyard could have spelled danger for Greta and Babette, so they were to play in the front yard and use the backyard only with adult supervision present. This plan actually worked well for Babette as she considered herself to be the mayor of the neighborhood. Nobody was a stranger to her. It was her job to greet the neighbors with a wiggle and a wink and befriend all neighborhood dogs, which she set about accomplishing immediately.

There was this basset hound named Wilber that weighed sixty pounds and was maybe two feet tall. His claim to fame was that he could dig under a fence like a backhoe regardless of the barriers the poor owners put up. He would drop by to visit, ears flopping almost to the ground and long snout sniffing while pointed to the air. He and Babette communicated across the fence about who knew what, with him leaving behind plenty of "Pee Mail." You could see Wilber thought Babette was a little hottie. One day, Wilber went the extra mile to impress her and tunneled under Babette's fence to romp together in the front yard. He would ever so often look to the sky and cut loose with a chesty-sounding bark that resembled an asthmatic without his inhaler.

Babette was more than a little boy crazy, and she didn't care who knew it. Wilber was dog-a-licious, but her hands down favorite fella was an enormously handsome, regal-looking black Great Dane named Hector. He stood four feet at the withers and presented a lithe, sculptured torso. No fence would turn him, and he would even show up at times with a light chain trailing from his collar, obviously snapped. He would tread backward for a couple of steps then leap over the five-foot chain-link fence in the front yard like it wasn't there. The two adored each other. Babette would coo and dance and lick his leg while he stood on point, soaking up the attention and wagging his tail majestically. She made a comical sight as she stood behind him on her hind legs, attempting to sniff his bottom. There was still easily three feet of space before she would even approximate her goal. One spring day, Kat checked on Babette in the front yard and found Hector asleep on Babette's pink outdoors blanket with Babette curled up on top of him. Babette loved her some Great Dane.

The neighborhood cats were not her friends however. They treated her with disrespect as they drank out of her water bowl and marked her personal territory with their deplorable scent. Rude! Unacceptable! If she caught one in her yard, she would give chase vigorously with a high-pitched bark. As cats aren't able to laugh out loud, nothing was actually audibly heard, but they would sneer at her until she was almost upon them then jump to the fence or the planter unconcernedly.

The kitty named Midnight was the worst. She was Babette's sworn nemesis. When Babette went out the doggy door, the first thing she did was search the yard for Midnight because whenever Midnight was present, Babette knew Midnight took a perverse pleasure in ridiculing Babette cruelly. She was a black bobtail alley cat with green eyes and a shiny coat who thought she was all that. Naturally, Babette felt obligated to keep Midnight in line; this was Babette's yard after all, so she chased her from one end of the yard to the other. Midnight would tread daintily across the top of the fence unhurriedly just in front of Babette, ignoring her. Often she would pointedly clean her coat, feigning indifference while Babette warbled from the ground. Occasionally, Midnight liked to mix it up by hopping down from the fence, taunting Babette like a matador does a bull then springing up lithely and gliding off like smoke when Babette got near. Insulting! Babette took it hard to be mocked so and charged across the lawn, always ready to kick some kitty butt. She never did catch Midnight but never tired of trying.

When she wasn't patrolling the front yard, Babette spent a good deal of time as the self-appointed nanny for Greta. She and Greta were inseparable. Greta grew into a beautiful toddler. She had a headful of golden curls. Her fragile features were offset by enormous aquamarine eyes fringed with her daddy's long lashes. The turned-up nose and bubble butt were features for which she could thank her mother. No one laid claim to the delicate rosebud lips, but Bob teased Kat by saying he seemed to remember a friend at the VFW who had very similar lips.

Everywhere Greta went, the little dog was in tow. Sometimes it wasn't the gentlest treatment from Greta as she would pull her ears or fur, but Babette acted as if it were a small price to pay and endured it selflessly. The only exception was if Greta would use those recently cut teeth to bite Babette's tail, to which Babette yelled for help but never took steps to rescue herself. If Babette happened to be dealing with the nefarious Midnight in the front yard and unavailable for play, Greta would look all over for her, babble a string of nonsense words, then call to her, "Baa-Baa," with a heavy accent on the second syllable.

Greta was tough to keep track of as she could toddle like lightning, if a bit unsteady. One afternoon, Kat could not find Greta. She searched the house, but Greta had vanished. "Greta, Greta," Kat called. "Ally, ally umpping free," she said, using the hide-and-seek call for "Come out, come out, wherever you are." No response. Eventually, on a whim, she checked the front yard. It turned out that Greta was safe and sound, having gone into the front yard after Babette through the doggy door. The two were enjoying playing in the mud, their eyes the only distinguishable feature on either of them. Now that Greta had learned that exit route, mom and dad were in deep trouble. You just couldn't unring that bell.

A fascinating plaything for which the two had a particular fondness was the bathroom. Kat tracked them down one day and found both Babette and Greta soaked—even Greta's hair was wet. Babette had somehow ended up in the toilet bowl and appeared to be unable to free herself. She had her front paws wrapped around the toilet seat like a life preserver. Toilet paper was strung all over the floor, across the hall, and plastered all over Greta. Toilet paper could be counted on for a good time. All that water and paper? Bathrooms were the best.

They shared everything, including food. Whatever Greta ate, she shared willingly with Babette—even such things as bananas and cooked carrots; these were not Babette's favorites, but she would force them down to be companionable. In turn, Greta had developed a real taste for kibble and had to be constantly supervised or would toddle straight for the dog food bowl and help herself. During her toddler years, dog food was a staple in Greta's diet.

When it came time for bed, Greta and Babette had a complex bedtime ritual. To say it was elaborate would be an understatement. First, Daddy came in to play a game called pinch and tickle. This game indeed involved a bit of tickling, but afterward, Daddy and Greta said their prayers together, which was rather the point. Then a sippy cup with water had to be tucked away in the corner of the crib. Each night, a story was read called *Are You My Mother?* in which a little girl had a pink tractor for a mama. Greta was a creature of habit, and though her parents tried to persuade her to read a different story, she stuck to her guns; it had to be *Are You My Mother?* Years later when asked what she would like to become when grown, she would reply, "A pink tractor."

Babette had her role in this nighttime ritual. According to Greta, Babette's tail contained mystical magic and could protect little girls from all manners of monsters, so Babette was handy to have around at night. Babette would inspect the closet, wagging her tail and barking on cue, which eradicated all the goblins residing there. Then apparently, there could be a malignant troll or two under the bed known as Waa-Waas, a sound Greta made that resembled the whirl of a vacuum cleaner but was used as a flexible term to mean anything Greta found frightening. Greta would point under the bed, nod her curly head, and utter, "Waa-Waa." To this, Babette would wag that magic tail and run under the crib and bark ferociously, thereby banishing anything threatening much to Greta's satisfaction.

At the end of these many steps, an exasperated Kat would kiss Greta good night and situate Babette at the foot of the crib in a clothes hamper. Just as Kat got comfortable in the living room with a book, *snap!* There was Greta, who had now figured out an avenue out of the crib, accompanied by Babette panting happily. So it came to be that the last step in the ever-expanding bedtime scenario included placing the chair that Greta used as her time-out chair in front of the bedroom door. "If you get out of that bed, Greta, you are going to get a time-out," Kat threatened.

That worked well for a couple of nights. One particular evening when Dad had tickled and said prayers, the cup was placed in the crib's corner, Babette had eradicated all the gruesome monsters, Kat read

Are You My Mother?, Greta got her good night kisses, and Kat retired to the living room, *bang!* Seconds later, in came Greta and Babette. "You forgot chair," Greta announced. Don't try to outsmart a toddler.

When they were performing this grand bedtime ritual at one point Babette appeared ill. She could not seem to sit still, running around in circles and shaking. She had never acted like this before, and while Kat had no idea why Babette might be frightened in this manner, it frankly alarmed her. Kat had grown to respect Babette's ability to sense danger. Was a member of their family in trouble? She wondered. She recalled Esmeralda's seizures. Could it be something like that? Then again, Kat had recovered from the gestational diabetes; as often happens, once the pregnancy was over, the high blood sugars normalize, but could her diabetes be back?

The other possibility was that Babette might genuinely be ill and need medical attention. Bob called her a worrywart and told her to come to bed, but she took a blanket into Greta's room and lay on the floor instead, staring worriedly at the ceiling.

Finally, at 2:30 AM in the morning, a tense Kat drifted off to sleep reluctantly. She awakened just thirty minutes later to Babette keening loudly and pawing her shoulder. She looked around concernedly, but Greta was sound asleep and safe. Five worried minutes later, the room began shaking and rolling with a loud bang. Dolls fell off the shelves, and the much-loved Tigger lamp crashed to the floor. The crib was scooting across the floor with its Tigger mobile dancing wildly. Greta awoke and began crying at the top of her lungs. Babette hopped around, standing on her hind legs and looking for a way to get into the hated crib to rescue her. Kat was screaming for Bob while she tried to stand in the face of all that movement. She was desperate to bring Greta to safety but could not find purchase. When it was over, Kat reached into the crib, pulling a terrified Greta into her arms and crooning softly, "It's all right, honey. It's all right." She sat back into the rocking chair that she used to rock Greta to sleep at night and gently stroked her head. Babette leaped into her lap and licked Greta's arm. Bob raced in to make certain no one was hurt, encircling his girls in his arms grateful to find them all three unharmed.

The next day, the TV had a field day. There was nothing like a good earthquake to breathe a little life into stale news. During the quake, the episode seemed like it went on interminably. But according to the ABC news team, the earthquake was a 6.2 on the Richter scale, the epicenter was indeed Fairfield, and the entire episode lasted a minute and thirty seconds. Bob surveyed the house for damage. There was a lot of breakage: vases cracked, knickknacks destroyed, potted plants smashed—just things though, really. "A free roller-coaster ride courtesy of the San Andreas Fault," he said with false joviality, trying to calm his girls.

California was the Promised Land in Bob and Kat's eyes. A sun-kissed paradise. The temperate weather, the diversity of terrain, and the easy, laid-back lifestyle. But for every rose, there are thorns, and earthquakes were undeniably a thorn to living in California. Not just anticipating and surviving the occasional ordeal but the necessity of dealing with that possibility influenced other aspects of life. For example, Bob had graduated with honors with his civil engineering degree in Arizona. He was prepared to work in a civil engineering capacity in Arizona without a hitch, but practicing in California required proof of competency in a specialized area unique to California called seismics, the study of structural design with regard to earthquakes. He would be held personally responsible to apply for and pass a five-hundred-dollar certification exam in structural earthquake engineering for reciprocity to practice in California as a civil engineer. Unfortunately, these courses had been omitted from the engineering program at Arizona State University as they were considered unnecessary to the area and so not part of the required curriculum. He would be given a grace period of two years to complete this requirement.

Always a self-starter, Bob purchased a *Seismic Review Manual* and began studying in the evenings. He popped for the five-hundred-dollar exam fee and took the exam as soon as it was available. Two weeks later, the notification came in the mail from the professional engineering board. He had failed the exam.

He broke out the manual and spent hours meticulously studying every Chapter. The couple scraped together the necessary five hundred dollars, and once again, he sat for the exam. Once again, he failed it. This was to happen three times. The notification would arrive, and Kat would dread the evening when Bob would come home to open the letter and find another failure. One day, as Kat was cleaning the bedroom, she glanced at Bob's dresser and noticed he had removed his ASU class ring. He later admitted to Kat that he no longer felt he deserved to wear it. Kat was heartbroken to see Bob so demoralized, but how could she help?

Kat learned more respect for Bob from these unfortunate failures than she had ever from his many successes. He did not give up but continued to study with renewed vigor. He just couldn't understand what he was missing. He looked around until he located a refresher course on the seismic requirement at UC Davis, which he paid for with another $250 dollars posted to the ailing MasterCard. After attending two of the three review classes, he came home one evening and said, "You know what? I was doing this all wrong. *No wonder* I couldn't pass the exam." When he next sat for the seismic exam, he went in with confidence and easily recognized what was needed on the test. He finished in half the allotted time and walked out whistling.

When he got home, Kat asked tentatively, "How'd it go?"

He thought it unwise to jinx it, so he said simply, "We'll see."

Two weeks later, Kat pulled the dreaded, familiar notice from the professional engineering board out of the mailbox and actually felt nauseated. It was a long day of anticipating Bob's arrival from work. She made a nice dinner and talked too much and laughed too loudly until after dinner when Bob said, "OK. Let's have it." He had known it came in all along. Kat handed Bob the letter and found something important to do in the kitchen, not wanting to see him devastated yet again. She stayed out of the room as long as she could tolerate then casually walked back in. There was Bob holding up his hand. The class ring was back on his ring finger where it belonged. He had passed with 97 percent—a victory hard-won.

From time to time, Kat reflected on Babette's reaction just prior to the recent earthquake. She was there as a witness and was positive that the little dog had sensed the impending quake as early as the night before. Checking online, she learned that the belief that animals successfully predict earthquakes has actually been around for centuries. According to an article in National Geographic, such accounts of similar anticipation of earthquakes are recorded as early as 373 BC. In September 2003, this same article references a medical doctor in Japan who made headlines with a study that indicated erratic behavior in dogs, such as barking or biting, can be used to accurately forecast earthquakes.

In fact, there is an entire body of animal psychology devoted to proving that dogs can predict earthquakes exceeding 6.0 on the Richter scale. Many, many people—believers, we call them—anecdotally relate incidents where dogs have foretold of an impending earthquake by their barking or shaking behaviors. You may not be among them, but as for Kat, she believed.

Chapter XII

THE BEACH IS A DANGEROUS PLACE

The family flourished during a truly golden era in their lives together. The neighborhood was like a warm hug with the couple making the types of friends that would last a lifetime. They established one lifelong friendship with a couple two doors down from them named Jeanine and Art. The friendship of the two families was one of those early friendships when young families are broke but inconceivably happy. Weekends were spent at each other's house eating dinner and playing cards or pool, with the kids watching TV together until they fell asleep in the spare room. One night, they played volleyball in the front yard together until 2:30 AM, having a blast and not feeling deprived about missing out on a fancy dinner but making their own fun instead.

Art and Jeanine were visual opposites. Jeanine was petite at just barely five feet tall and maybe weighed one hundred pounds soaking wet. She had long, curly brunet hair that looked massive on her tiny frame and sported a constant smile. Art was a hulking giant of a man, weighing in at over 220 pounds and standing six feet five. People would gasp when he walked into a room, and the first question was always "Just how tall are you?" His standard answer was seventy-seven inches, giving them pause as they calculated. He was a police officer and looked the part with a shock of thick black hair, a bushy mustache to match, and a perpetual scowl worn on his face. He always seemed a little sullen and a little dangerous, which maybe wasn't so far from the truth. He had actually gained a sort of local notoriety when a lowlife had gone into Pizza Land last year and shot two children then escaped. Art answered the call as a first responder and held one of the victims, a four-year-old girl, while she died in his arms crying for her daddy. Art relentlessly tracked the murderer down and killed him in an exchange of gunfire, earning him the nickname of the Grizzly. It was something he avoided talking about except to say, with a steely glint in his eyes, he would do it again in a heartbeat.

Art and Jeanine had a son six months older than Greta named Trevor. This six months that Trevor had on Greta was a card he played often during spats as proof that those six months made him older and hence smarter. Greta loved Trevor. During the years, their friendship had its ups and downs, as friendships will. There was the awful hair-pulling and biting incident where no was hurt but both were bitten. And of course, there were those altercations when things were said that neither child meant. Sometimes these episodes even degenerated into obscene five-year-old-type cuss words and name-calling. Terms such as *pooh-pooh head* were bandied about in the heat of the moment. In the face of it all though, the friendship abounded.

Both couples loved the beach, so they planned a rare vacation—a camping trip together to Sunset Beach with their new (used but new to them) pop-up trailer. They would stay on the cliffs above Sunset Beach, party at Santa Cruz Boardwalk, swim in their beloved Pacific Ocean, and eat crab on Fisherman's Wharf in San Francisco.

The trek began one Saturday morning with the couples each taking separate cars. A tow hitch had been added to Kat's classic red Mustang convertible for the tent trailer. They dropped the top on the Mustang convertible and embarked on their trip with Babette and Greta snuggled in the backseat.

The trip was enjoyable and uneventful until they pulled in to the state park at Sunset Beach. Apparently, there was more to these pop-up trailer setups than the people who had sold the trailer let on. The camping site had a bit of a decline that had to be accounted for, or the camper would slide downhill precariously. They bungled through the setup, both men trying to level the camper and set up the propane stove with feigned bravado. That evening, though, the details of the fine art of camping reared its ugly head on the unprepared foursome. No one had matches. Really? No matches? Also, none of these camping geniuses had considered a lantern a thing of necessity. A fellow camper, parked next to them, took pity on them and gave them some matches. They had only campfire light that night. Stumbling around for a nighttime visit to the locally situated community bathroom was accomplished with light from those precious matches only. The next day, they shopped at the Clearancemart Department store with a new respect for camping gear in general and matches in particular.

Santa Cruz Boardwalk was a ball. The kids were both five now, an age where the roller coaster, tame by Magic Mountain standards, was just thrilling enough. Bob and Greta boarded the roller coaster with Greta beaming. As the coaster started out, Greta raised her hands to the sky and shouted, "*Holy—*" Oops. Bob was acquainted with this term and worried about the next word to escape her young mouth, but in the end, what she said was "Guacamole." It was a day filled with fun. Greta even got a temporary henna tattoo on her right shoulder that said, "Daddy's girl." A great day was had by all—even the leashed Queen Babette who held court with the crowd on the boardwalk.

At sunset, the entire campground filed to the cliffs to watch the glory for which the beach was named as the sun sank in the western sky. The panoramic view included the broad expanse of the ice-blue Pacific Ocean, waves crashing to shore, and a clear view of the curvature of the earth detectable from this vantage point. The couples sat, with the little ones perched on their laps, breathless at the majesty, the sky glowing golden red and fading gradually to lavender as the night peeked over the horizon.

In the mornings, the two families would pack up whatever they felt was needed for the day, descend the cliff using the long stairs provided, and set up their picnic area for the day. Babette was permitted on the beach provided she was leashed, according to the park ranger, but once on the beach, she had free reign and nobody objected. She was enthralled with the sand, digging holes and frolicking, but she was not going in that briny water. She would go up to a wave then scamper back dry to the shaded blanket. She watched people go in like they were crazy but considered herself too intelligent to get wet like that in the churning sea. She didn't get it.

The two families spent long, lazy days on the beach, soaking up the sun and just spending time together. Art found a sand dollar, opened it, and told the kids the sand dollar legend that he had memorized as a kid:

The Sand Dollar Legend

Upon this odd-shaped seashell, a legend grand is told
about the life of Jesus, that wondrous tale of old.
At its center, you will see there seems to be a star
like the one that led the shepherds and wise men from afar.
Around its surface are the marks of nails and thorns and spear
suffered by Christ upon the cross; the wounds show plainly here.

But there is also an Easter lily clear for us to see,
the symbol of Christ's resurrection for all eternity.

Art loomed like a giant over Greta and Trevor while reciting the poem and showing them where the designs were located on the sand dollar. The kids were in awe and could be heard reciting a resonable facsimile of the legend while they dug in the sand or played a game of cars at Trevor's insistence. The next morning, Art promised each child a dime for every sand dollar they could beach comb, and in a couple of days, they had accumulated nearly five dollars, which in the end was devoted to their ice cream habit. Art was a good parent and a teddy bear, not a grizzly bear in many ways where those he loved were concerned.

During the day, the adults took turns watching the kids while the others waded out into the waves, swam, and bodysurfed until they were exhausted. They always ate lunch on the beach, and then in the evening, they built a fire, roasted chicken or hot dogs on the spit and then marshmallows, and told ghost stories. Greta's favorite was the one about the haunted tent trailer that had a good ghost in residence who lived in the dark because there were no matches.

The kids were toast by the end of the day after swimming all day and marching up and down that long flight of stairs. There were no arguments or exorbitant rituals for bedtime. They were crying to go to sleep. After they went down, the adults got serious about drinking beer and playing pinochle, which they kept up until two in the morning. Maybe it wasn't vacationing in the Bahamas like some other people, but to these good friends and their children, it was the best vacation ever.

The final morning of their stay at Sunset, they packed to go down to the beach to spend the day. They lugged everything down the stairs and claimed their usual spot, setting up the umbrella and putting out the sand toys.

At times, there were unavoidable trips back up that godforsaken hill for forgotten items, like there was that morning. When they realized nobody brought sunblock, the four adults played rock, paper, scissors to see who would scale that set of steps for sun block and, since they were going, to replenish the beer. So it was that this time, Kat lost. "I knew I should have used rock," she mumbled as she resigned herself to the climb. "Watch Greta," she yelled to Jeanine, who nodded in acknowledgement, and Kat began the ascent.

The youngsters were busy fashioning a castle extraordinaire complete with a moat and turrets. Babette contributed by alternately digging holes and crawling into their laps covered with sand. The two men were competing for the best waves as they bodysurfed. Jeanine watched the kids like it was her only ambition in life.

This was when Babette started acting up. She began barking and pawing at the kids with typical "Timmy in the well" behavior. Greta brushed her off, saying, "Get down, Babette. Quit." Babette persisted. She continued barking, and this time, she growled. Babette? Growl? At Greta? Yes, it was so. Jeanine watched in amazement at this uncharacteristic behavior. Then something happened that was so startling that Greta just could not believe it. Babette reached over, nipped Greta on the hand, and set off running. Greta stood up to give chase. Babette had crossed the line; nipping was not tolerated. But as Greta followed her in pursuit, Babette dove in the water. Shocked because Greta was well aware of Babette's position on swimming in the ocean, she waded in after her even though she was angry. What if her little Babette drowned? When she reached Babette, she stumbled into something in the water. Convinced she had bumped into a shark, she quickly looked down and was startled to see her father under the water. Shock registered, and instinctively she reached down and pulled him up by his hair, the only thing she could reach. Upon breaking the surface, he gasped air. His face was bright red. He had a five-by-five-inch abrasion on the center of his forehead. She held him up with one hand and trapped Babette under the other arm. Oddly, he seemed unable to stand, and the three were buffeted by the waves. Greta began pulling both to safety as best she could. When the wave went out and the water was shallow enough, Bob was able to get to his knees but not stand. Jeanine had reached the water by then and took a sopping-wet Babette from Greta. Greta continued to grasp her father by his left arm, and Jeanine took his right arm. The right arm was curled tightly against his chest, his right fist in a ball. He tried to stand on his left leg, which seemed strong, but could not bear weight on his right. Together Jeanine and Greta hauled Bob out of the ocean, dragging him to shore. He was vomiting water and pulling air into his lungs hungrily.

Kat was about halfway down the hated steps when she saw her dear husband pulled onto the shore by her tiny five-year-old daughter. She dropped the beer and took the stairs two and three at a time, her heart racing. From this distance, she could not be certain if he was alive or dead. "Please, God. Please, God," she repeated, terror coursing through her body. By the time she reached him, Bob was beginning to breathe easier. She gathered him in her arms and kissed his face. "It's OK, sweetheart," she crooned. "You're OK. I got you." He lay there unable to respond. "Get a blanket," she ordered.

Jeanine retrieved a beach towel, laying it over him and watching him intently. They remained in this position for a very long time. No one spoke. No one moved. They were oblivious to the people walking the shoreline who skirted around them. Kat held Bob close to her as she cried and prayed with her family and friends beside her.

Eventually, Bob was able to uncurl his right hand and straighten his fingers slowly. His right arm was still rigid. Kat was ready to call for help. Then eventually, he could partially extend his right arm. He assured her he was fine, though a skeptical Kat was not persuaded. They helped him to limp/hop on his left foot to the blanket at his insistence. He fell asleep draped with beach towels. Nobody swam. They all just watched and waited on alert to call paramedics. When he woke, he was able to extend his right arm. He tried tentatively to stand on his right leg, but it felt weak, and he sat back down. The next attempt, he was able to bear weight but limped while favoring his right leg. Steadily he was regaining strength. They dared to hope that he was recovering.

A lifeguard was located who could transport Bob up the cliff on a service road in his jeep. Bob improved as the night wore on, but nobody had much in the way of vacation spirit left, so the trip was cut short by two days, blowing off the excursion to San Francisco they had planned. Bob was quiet and reflective, as was Kat. She thought about what life without Bob would have been like and whether she and Greta could have gone on without him. She couldn't imagine it. She didn't want to imagine it. But she knew this was a close call.

"What happened, honey?" Kat asked later.

Bob told of the pleasant afternoon of bodysurfing. He and Art had goaded each other on to be more and more daring, watching for the grandest waves to challenge. They were catching some magnificent waves. A monster loomed over the horizon, and Bob set out to catch it just right, hoping to arrive victoriously all the way to the shore. He caught the wave but was slammed forward headfirst under the water, hitting the ground hard with his forehead then flipping over. He felt his neck hyperextend then pop and was powerless to fight to a standing position. He was trapped underwater, staring up at the sunlight above. He thought to himself that this was his end. God was calling him home.

"It's true," Bob said to Kat. "The high points of your life flash before you."

He recalled the first time he met Kat. He remembered acting nonchalant, but he knew that day that she was the girl he would marry. He visualized Kat's look of determination the day she first whisked a dying puppy from his hands. Also, he saw the first time he held his perfect little daughter in his arms as a newborn infant. He replayed his graduation day in his mind—when he had earned his civil engineering degree and, more importantly, his father's respect. He thought to himself, *I have been so fortunate.* As he felt his oxygen dwindling, he desperately looked to the safety of the surface and was surprised to see a dog-paddling Babette swimming above his head. It was then that Greta reached for him and pulled him to the surface for that life-giving gasp of breath. His five-year-old daughter with the help of Babette had saved his life. Babette had paid him back for the day he whisked her away from a watery death so long ago.

Chapter XIII

MAYBE IT IS A DOG'S WORLD

On the ride back to Fairfield from Sunset Beach, Bob slept soundly in the backseat, convertible top up on the Mustang. Greta was in Jeanine's car in the backseat, fighting with Trevor like a couple of cranky old married people.

Babette had commandeered the shotgun seat so she could front-seat drive and stick her head out the window. Kat stroked the fluffy little dog with great affection. Babette looked up at Kat with one of her world-class dog smiles. Kat said to her, "OK, Babette, how did you pull this one off?"

Greta tattled on Babette for nipping her. She even had the faint teeth marks to prove it. Kat believed this was a last-ditch attempt on Babette's part to get Greta's attention, and of course, it worked. Babette went into the despised salty water in spite of her fear with no regard for her own safety and somehow guided Greta to Bob's precise location. He was not visible and could not be detected by scent as he was underwater, so how was this even possible? It's not like she could visualize his location within the churning sea. Had the rescue effort been even slightly delayed, at best Bob might have been paralyzed. At worst, Kat would have been a widow and Greta would had faced growing up fatherless. It was nothing short of a miracle.

Kat peered into the furry, contented face, searching Babette's eyes for something. Maybe a spark of clairvoyance? ESP? Intuition?

Extraordinary intelligence? Anything to explain why Babette was able to do what seemed impossible.

We humans believe we are at the top of the food chain. We are sufficiently arrogant to think that all other animals are somehow inferior to us—that our opposable thumbs, speech, and gift of recall grant us license to smugly dominate over every other life-form. Today's research gives us pause to ponder the veracity of that premise.

We are developing a new respect for dogs in the face of conclusive studies that confirm dogs have a far-greater intelligence level than we had previously given them credit. In an article found online on the website   animals.howstuffworks.com/pets/dogs-understand-words.htm, Jane McGrath presents evidence that shows it is possible for a dog to comprehend as many as two hundred words, right up there with the vocabulary of a three-year-old child, based on a border collie named Rico. Rico knew the names of each of his playthings and would correctly fetch the toy requested. Certainly, a command like "Go find Mommy and give her a kiss" is a doable task for a dog with a command of this many words.

Consider just the canines' superior sense of smell. In an article published by Alabama and Auburn Universities (www.aces.edu), in the nasal cavity of a dog, there are minimally 220 million receptors responsible for identifying scent. This keen sense of smell has been tested, and researchers report that canines can accurately identify bladder cancer, lung cancer, breast cancer, epileptic seizures, abnormal blood sugars of a diabetic, and even infections such as E. coli. No human can hope to recognize diseases with the sense of smell. In our wildest imagination, we only surmise how this translates into other canine capabilities not yet recognized by science.

Unlike humans, dogs have great night vision because of a reflective structure in the back of their eyes called a tapetum. This structure acts like a mirror to enhance their ability to capture light, enabling them to see in five-times-dimmer light than a human and giving them superior visibility in all levels of light. Nocturnal hunting, self-preservation, and protection of the pack are all enhanced by their far-superior night vision.

We maintain that humans domesticated dogs—which made them stupid, docile pets—but according to a book by Brian Hare and Vanessa Woods entitled *The Genius of Dogs*, the reverse may be true. Humans selectively bred dogs with an affinity for humans as well as those with superior senses that overcame the difficulties encountered in the environment. According to a quote provided by *The Genius of Dogs* from Colin Groves of the Australian National University, it was dogs who domesticated us:

Dogs acted as humans' alarms system, trackers and hunting aides, garbage disposal facilities, hot water bottles and children's guardian and playmates. Humans provided dogs with food and security . . . Humans domesticated dogs and dogs domesticated humans.

Could it be that dogs are in many ways the superior being to humans? Superior senses: sense of smell, improved night vision, excellent hearing. With all the seemingly magical abilities those acute senses afford them, what if they are simply too evolved and noble to use their superiority to take advantage of us? They have the potential to hunt in packs armed with a keen sense of smell and hearing but, rather than competing with humans, have been content to humbly serve instead with quiet dignity? *Could it be that Babette is the pack leader and we are her pack?*

Still more incredible was Babette's apparently advanced capabilities compared to the average dog. Perhaps Babette's early brush with drowning as a newborn puppy could explain the psychic feats? Maybe the oxygen deprivation was long enough to change the brain chemically, enabling her to perform on a level most dogs cannot? There are countless stories of people who had near-death experiences, who gazed into that tantalizing "white light," and were never the same. People laid claim to new powers like ESP or laying on of hands, a gift of healing by touching as a result of narrowly escaping death and cheating the reaper.

Kat really had no idea how Babette was able to do some of the things that she did. Her personal theory was one she held close to her heart. Was it possible that Babette was Godsent? A sort of little guardian angel who guided the family through the land mines of life? Surely, anyone looking into the face of a dog to see the unquestioning, selfless love could sense the hand of God. If indeed, as people say, everything happened for a reason in a predestined fashion, then Babette's minor miracles might be explained as divine intervention. It was as plausible and maybe more plausible than any other explanation.

A favorite quote by Einstein came to her mind, one that Kat clung to often:

The most beautiful thing we can experience is the mysterious. It is the source of all true art and science. He to whom the emotion is a stranger, who can no longer pause to wonder and stand wrapped in awe is as good as dead—his eyes are closed. The insight into the mystery of life, coupled though it be with fear, has also given rise to religion. To know what is impenetrable to us really exists, manifesting itself as the highest wisdom and radiant beauty, which our dull faculties can comprehend only in their most primitive forms—this knowledge, this feeling is at the center of true religiousness.

From super spiritual to supernatural, another possibility that Kat pondered was that the ability was not Babette's but Kat's. Kat had heard of cases where an individual considered their home to be haunted and relocated to another house only to find that the odd events moved with them. It wasn't the house; it was the individual.

Or the poltergeist phenomena, an example of a paranormal experience haunting a person rather than a place. These chilling manifestations include articles being hurled in the air, noises, breakage, and occasionally, actual and petty physical attacks. The origin is thought to be the person themselves, such as a young girl during her transition to womanhood. A kind of transference.

Kat discussed this theory later with her friend Jeanine that possibly Babette was getting a sort of power boost from the close relationship between Babette and her "pack." Jeanine told Kat that she had seen the truth of such paranormal things when her mother died in Massachusetts five years before. Jeanine awoke at 3:00 AM to see her mother standing at the edge of the bed and smiling down at her. She called her father at the home she left in Massachusetts when she married Art. In a hailstorm of emotion, her father told her that her mother died in her sleep an hour ago. This amazing visitation from her departed mother Jeanine attributed to the close relationship between her mother and herself, and accordingly, she believed in the wonder of such things.

For Kat, there *was* one unexplained, twilight zone-like incident. It was so emotional and mystical that she had shared it willingly with no one, knowing that it would be met with skepticism. Certainly, *she* wouldn't have believed it if she hadn't witnessed it. If Jeanine could trust her with that preposterous "dead mother at the foot of the bed" story, then Kat could share her one incredible story with Jeanine.

In her early teens, Kat had a crush on a guy that starred in one of those garage bands, like a lot of budding musicians in their early years. His name was Charles, but he called himself Harley—way cooler. He enjoyed natural good looks; according to the junior high groupies, he was babe-a-licious with an awesome body and bedroom eyes. He was the kind that didn't even have to try. He used swear words to punctuate every sentence; he strutted and flipped his long, shaggy blond hair when he walked and was over-the-top popular. Harley was the lead singer in a teenage rock-and-roll band, and Kat was Harley's chick. Having a garage band granted the instant prestige of a minor deity in junior high. It guaranteed the one most important thing at this age: acceptance among peers. The two were reigning royalty, the John F. and Jackie Kennedy of middle school, and enjoyed their undisputed position in the in crowd.

Their band was new and still in the early stages of organization, but at least they had agreed on a name: the Plastic Skulls. They'd been together for six months and had found boys to fill all the positions for guitars, drums, and of course, lead singer. Making Harley lead singer was a no-brainer since he already had an almost-cult following at the junior high school. They hadn't had a gig yet, but they were working on it, practicing as often as they could. They accomplished these practice sessions by rotating from one band member's house to the next. One set of parents would tolerate the noise for as long as humanly possible, and then in theory, it was the next boy in the band's turn to play too loudly at their house.

Jeremy was the newest member of the Plastic Skulls. He was painfully shy and cursed with out-of-control acne, a double whammy in junior high school where cruelty ruled the day. Being a complete nerd and probably not the most talented drummer, if the truth were told, he came by his position almost by default—he brought to the table a place to practice. His parents were either particularly tolerant or completely tone-deaf, so most times if there was no other option, the Skulls would screech and play off-key there at Jeremy's basement. It was his ticket into the world of junior high status and likely his only shot at it.

Jeremy's house was well suited to sustain the audible assault because it was a large, sprawling two-story house. The bottom story was an enormous soundproofed recreation/guest quarters. It had been set up as a media center with a projector TV complete with large roll-down screen, speakers in the walls, and lots of sofas and beanbag chairs scattered all over—a Mecca for teenagers who were looking to score a hangout.

Classic rock posters were hung all over the walls. A gorgeous James Dean stared down with tragic, sultry eyes. One could not look into the poster without thinking of his early death. Another poster featured a wailing Janice Joplin caught midsong, belting out some rock-and-roll oldie with eyes squinting and knuckles white on the microphone. Jimmie Hendricks was portrayed; if you closed your eyes, you could imagine you heard him crooning, "Are you experienced?" The Doors smiled back from a group picture of the band—and others. As Kat took notice, she realized all the rock stars in the posters had experienced an untimely or drug-influenced death. Hmmmm. When Kat thought about it, it seemed more creepy than inspirational for the young musicians.

A long set of steps led down from the upstairs living quarters to the basement, emptying into a lengthy hall that ended in an exit door. On the one side of the wall was the long open recreation room, where the boys set up their microphones, speakers, and instruments. On the other side of the hall were three furnished guest bedrooms, each with its own bathroom. The guest bedrooms were good sized. They were furnished identically: a queen-size bed, dresser, basement-type window, and its own powder room with a shower only—no tub. They were decorated in sedate colors: cool blues, beiges, and soft pastel-yellow tones.

As Harley's chick, Kat was expected to attend each jam session and look adoringly at Harley as he bellowed. This was the requirement if you wanted the E ticket of being Harley's girl. She considered it her due, and so she paid the price as long as she could, but everyone had their limits.

Often when the earplugs failed and the aspirin ran out, Kat would sneak out of the recreation room and steal upstairs where she tapped softly on the door to the first floor to visit with Jeremy's mother, Agatha. She had a lovely stillness that made Kat think of a doe in a forest. She was a tall, willowy woman with tawny hair and smoky green eyes. Agatha was considered hip by Jeremy's circle of friends. Word on the street was that Jeremy's parents smoked pot, which earned them a special place in the hearts of the in crowd. Beyond that was the fact that Jeremy's mom was always receptive to a troubled teen. She was a soft place to land, a shoulder to cry on, and a sounding board for a lost teenager traveling a self-destructive path.

Jeremy had a younger brother, Davy, who was three years old. He had been born two and a half months premature, almost like Agatha's body had made the hard decision for her. Despite the rocky beginning, modern science rescued the infant only to discover he had a constellation of severe congenital birth defects. Davy was born blind, deaf, and seriously ill in other ways like heart and lung problems. He was undersized for his age, more the size of a year-old toddler, giving him an elfin quality. He had beautiful, straight pale-blond hair that looked like someone put a bowl on his head to guide his haircut. It cascaded around him like a waterfall when he turned. Because he could not communicate, it was nearly impossible to predict his level of intelligence, but he was enormously affectionate and could both identify and locate people he adored. By smell? Kat couldn't imagine how he was able to do this.

In the face of impossible odds, Davy circumvented his handicaps and was able to function on an impossibly high level: He could feed himself, was potty trained, rode a tricycle, knew the layout of the house, and had a method for navigating by using his hands to slap against the sides of the walls. These were high standards by which to judge any three-year-old boy, let alone one working with severe handicaps. Davy and Kat were devoted to each other. True to her spirit as a future nurse, she reached out lovingly to the little boy with pity in her heart. As the two bonded, that pity was replaced by sheer amazement at the advanced functioning Davy demonstrated.

Agatha would respond to Kat's knock when she snuck out of band practice with a welcoming smile and a hug, inviting her to share a cup of tea. Agatha always had an array of exotic teas, often purchasing them especially to share with Kat. She had purchased a tropical coconut blend for the next time she would see Kat and told her so when she opened the door. Once seated at the kitchen table together with large mugs of steaming, aromatic tea, Davy was somehow alerted that Kat was there. He raced down the hall, slapping the sides of the wall to guide him to the kitchen and having arrived, sailed into Kat's arms, showering her with wet kisses. It was the best part of Kat's week to cradle Davy in her arms while he searched her face with her hands, a smile on his face to melt a glacier.

Kat and Davy played together whenever she was there. He loved to go downstairs to the room where the band was jamming. He obviously could not "hear" the music but danced just the same, faithful to the beat that Kat guessed was gauged by the vibration of the music. Before going back upstairs to Agatha, Kat and Davy would detour to one of the guest rooms on the other side of the hall. He would slap the walls to guide him to the room of his choice. The two scrambled to the bed and bounced and jumped on the mattress together, holding hands and laughing.

A sad thing happened. Davy began succumbing to the heart problem with which he came into the world. He had dealt courageously with the impact of a bad heart, adapting in many ways, but fatigue dominated his day as his heart failed to compensate. It was depressing to watch the once-bouncy Davy struggle to walk across the floor and wasting away daily. One day, Kat got the news at school that Davy lost the fight. He died the night before in an ICU with his parents and Jeremy present. She felt like the spark that lit her world had been stolen from her. Her grief was a wild animal gnawing at her heart.

For a long time, Kat could not attend the weekly caterwauling that passed for band practice. The Skulls had worn their welcome thin at the other boys' homes and had to rely on Jeremy's parents' goodwill for a place to practice. Kat was still mourning Davy's loss herself and couldn't yet imagine comforting Agatha without breaking down. When she felt she could be supportive to Agatha emotionally, she finally went back into Jeremy's house.

She endured the pounding, discordant music, trying to gird herself up to mount the stairs and tap on the upstairs door to express her condolences to Agatha. She stepped into the hall with the intention to lighten Agatha's grief by sharing her burden. She planned to hold her and give her the chance to remember Davy with a safe person who could empathize with her grief (Kat loved Davy too) but was distant enough not to be devastated by her pain. She put one foot on the staircase and grabbed the banister when inexplicably she heard the all-too-familiar slapping sound that Davy used to make when navigating the house. It was descending the staircase toward her. The hair on the back of her neck stood up as the slapping sound got closer and closer. She didn't think but responded instinctually with a primal reaction. She turned on her heel and began running down the hallway toward the exit door, the slapping sound following closely behind her. She seemed to be running in slow motion, syrupy seconds lasting forever, and making no progress. As she passed the first bedroom, she could hear the noise of someone bouncing on the bed, and she thought she could hear giggling—giggling the way Davy used to giggle. She passed the next bedroom at a full sprint and could hear the same sound; this time, she turned to look at the bed and could see that the mattress bouncing up and down, like it would if someone were bouncing on the bed, but nobody was there. She was really sprinting now. She sped past the third bedroom; everything was clearer. She could hear the giggling and the bouncing and could see the mattress springing up and down with clarity. She reached the end of the hall and bounded through the exit door. Kat never returned to that house after that.

It had been awhile since Kat had thought about that incident. The day this occurred, there were many people there, yet she was the only one to have had that encounter with Davy. She explored how she felt about the incident. Terrified? Yes, because it exceeded that which she knew of as accepted scientific boundaries, but certainly, it was not anything that she sensed as evil. A great remorse hit her afresh at the loss of Davy—so unique an individual, so rare. Though for all her sadness, she was grateful for the entire experience because it taught her that there exists magic in the world beyond her ken. That was the closest she could come to the realm of the supernatural, but it opened up for her the world of wonder. It granted her permission to be a believer.

Maybe Kat would never know a surefire explanation for Babette's feats, but that did not make them any less real. She marveled that Babette had rescued Bob from the ocean under the circumstances that it happened. She looked for evidence of other accounts of what might only be considered canine sixth sense. What she found was that there were scores of such anecdotes. Like the one featured on Petside.com:

This article proclaims the family's black Labrador, Bear, to be nothing short of a hero. The story goes that Patricia Drauch—mother to her fourteen-month-old son, Stanley—did not notice that he had taken off while she was gardening in the front yard. But Bear certainly did. Bear circled to the backyard. There was Stanley facedown in the pool. Bear leaped into the pool to save the drowning toddler. By the time Stanley was found to be missing, Bear had swum him to safety. Mrs. Drauch called the paramedics, and the child was transported to the hospital for examination. To his parents' great relief, he was discharged the same day—physically sound and unharmed. Explain that, you nonbelievers.

Chapter XIV

SCHOOL DAYS

Fall rolled around, and Fairfield was shrouded in the magnificence of falling orange and red leaves. The weather settled down, the blistering heat quickly succumbing to a welcomed coolness in the air. With the arrival of autumn, the first day of school loomed, and Greta and Trevor anticipated the experience with a mixture of excitement and dread. Trevor had an abundance of theories on just what was in store for them. He was happy to share his ideas with Greta. One of the more imaginative theories had something to do with a dragon for which the kids were tasked with feeding and walking. Greta objected to this strenuously and asked if Kat could write a note to her teacher that excused her from dragon duty. In the end, Kat thought, *What the heck?* She wrote out the note, and Greta carefully carried it to school and gave it to her teacher on the first day of school. Let the teacher figure it out.

The day came. Trevor picked up Greta on the way to school, and the two mothers planned to walk with them, meet the teacher, and commiserate on the way home over losing their babies. Greta had on a brand-new pink dress, her long blond hair pulled into pigtails with pink bows. Trevor actually pulled out all the stops and spiked his hair using Megagel Mousse. He was a fine figure of a kindergartner in his new jeans and Vans tennis shoes.

Babette went along on a leash. She didn't know where she was going, but she was overjoyed to take a walk at this time of the day. She was flabbergasted at the number of children who all walked to the same destination. A veritable smorgasbord of children—Babette's favorite people. She was torn in all directions to play with as many of the willing boys and girls as possible. They walked to the end of the block and entered the back door of Mount Washington Elementary School, crossing the baseball fields and passing backstops on their way to the kindergarten rooms. There were three connected kindergarten rooms with back doors that led to a fenced play yard separated from the big kids' play area.

Greta and Trevor were disappointed to find they were in separate rooms, Greta in Ms. Toney's class and Trevor next door in Mr. Garcia's. At least they could look forward to playing together at recess, which gave them a certain sense of security. The mothers gathered into the kindergarten classrooms to meet the teachers and each other. Babette was over the top, greeting everyone with a modest Do the Babette number that universally enchanted the group, children's mothers, and teacher. Reluctantly, Jeanine and Kat dropped off their youngsters and turned to retrace the steps they had taken to get to school. They mused on how this could have happened. Just yesterday the little ones were the major part of every waking moment. What if they got scared? What if one of the other kids teased them and hurt their feelings? Letting them go, to sink or swim, to take their medicine where life was concerned was tough on the moms—all three of them.

Babette was disconcerted to leave the school without her kids and staged a formal protest. The moms had mistakenly left the youngsters at the school, and Babette meant to make them aware of this awful mistake. She dug in her heels and refused to walk. She pulled at the leash, heading back toward the kindergarten classrooms. The moms were callously ignoring her, so she fell back on the whining thing, which generally was surefire, but no. What could they be thinking? They forgot the kids. Kat had little choice but to pick Babette up and carry her forcibly back to the house with her squirming to get free the whole time.

Upon arriving at the house, Kat placed Babette back on the ground in the front yard and swung the gate closed. Babette was outraged. How could Kat forget Babette's little girl? Where was Greta? Was she all right? Babette gave it one more college try, whining and staring at the gate and running back and forth the length of the fence. Kat offered her treats and tried to pet her to calm her, but Babette wasn't having any. Kat eventually gave up, and so did Babette but not for a long, long time. She fell asleep exhausted by the front gate.

At noon, Kat clipped the leash to Babette's collar and started back down the block toward the elementary school, picking up Jeanine on the way. Babette saw hope and led Kat down the street at a dead run with her short legs pumping. Kindergarten classes were letting out just as they arrived at the classrooms, and Greta and Trevor met in front, chattering excitedly about their day. Babette was in ecstasy. She wiggled, danced, and winked like she had never done before. Her kids, she had her kids back. She pranced happily all the way back to the house, tongue lolling. The rest of the day, Greta couldn't get two feet away without Babette hunting her down. Kat knew the next day of school would be the same horrible day for Babette.

Kat hoped that Babette would eventually adjust to the fact that Greta had to be in school during the day. The two women walked to school together in the mornings with Babette and the youngsters, but Babette reacted to the separation with the same severe reaction. It was fresh hell for her every time. She would not come into the house or eat until Greta was back for the day. Kat felt sorry for the anxious Babette; she was despondent.

One day, she peeked outside expecting to see Babette guarding the front gate where she spent her days during school. She was not there. In fact, Kat scoured the house and both the back and front yards, but she was not anywhere. Looking to the gate, Kat noticed there was a hole dug under the fence. She grabbed her keys and called Jeanine to help search for Babette, but they could not find her. It was time to pick up the kids from school anyway, so the two women walked to the kindergarten classes. As the classroom let out, here came Greta and Trevor, and lo and behold, there was a happy Babette with her most winning dog smile. "Just what are you doing here, missy?" Kat asked. Babette did a rendition of Do the Babette, but Kat was not taken in by her charm. "You're in big trouble," Kat said.

Ms. Toney told Kat that Babette had been found barking on the outside of the kindergarten fence. Ms. Toney had brought her inside the classroom to keep her safe. "But Babette can't come to school every day," she said. "We didn't get a thing done except petting her."

Kat felt like she was in grade school again at risk for detention and assured Ms Toney it wouldn't happen again. But it did.

It got to the point where Kat couldn't let Babette outside while Greta was at school or she'd be out that fence like a shot. They tried putting rocks along the fence to discourage her from digging. Even so, incredibly, Babette seemed to find a way out. One day, the phone rang.

When Kat answered it, she found the principal of Mount Washington Elementary, Mr. Bailey, on the line. "Come get her," he said. "Oh, by the way, this time she was found on the playground with an enormous Great Dane in her company. You don't know who he belongs to, do you?" It wasn't enough that Babette got herself into trouble; she was leading Hector down a criminal path too.

Chapter XV

THE WAA-WAA

Once Babette had discovered that she could win her freedom by digging under the fence, she was unstoppable, rocks or no rocks. There was some talk of blaming Wilber—that somehow this idea was taught to her by Wilber since he actually did dig under the fence at one point, and Babette was nothing if not a quick study. But to be fair to Wilber, there was that history in Arizona of her digging under a fence of her own accord when the necessity arose. It got so that she was a demon once she escaped through the doggy door. The tunneling under the fence was fueled by her great desire to protect Greta who was being neglectfully abandoned at school by her mother. Mom must have been losing her grip. Babette had little choice but to step in. She had gotten this "tunneling under the fence" thing down to a science and found that if she applied her technique, the hole only maybe took a speedy ten minutes to dig tops.

Bob and Kat were at a loss on how to prevent Babette from digging under the fence. Certainly, it was a dangerous practice. She could be hit by a car, attacked by another dog, lost, or stolen. And Mr. Bailey, the principal at the school, was starting to lose his sense of humor about her appearances. Something had to be done.

They talked of many solutions. Bob even suggested to a horrified Kat that Babette be tethered on a light chain to a stake in the ground. One look at Kat's "icky" face convinced Bob that was a bad idea. Bob called that look "icky face" because he recognized that scrunched up frown as a signal that an argument was in his immediate future.

Keeping Babette inside the house and allowing her outside only when she was leashed could work. The problem was that Babette spent most of her indoor time scratching at the door when Greta was gone, so no one could be sure if it was out of a need to relieve herself or the desire to charge that fence and take a trip down to the elementary school. Consequently, Kat took many unscheduled, unnecessary walks with Babette, which got old fairly fast. Also, what if nature called and no one was home to take her out?

"What about covering the pool and keeping her in the backyard?" Bob offered. Most of the space in the backyard was taken up by the pool, with a couple of crowded planters and no grassy areas. No place really for Babette to relieve herself except on the deck. Plus, it was just plain dangerous because in a split second, Babette might fall through the cover or make her way into the backyard when the cover was not in place. It didn't seem to be an ideal solution to the problem at hand.

They had talked before about building a little courtyard in the front yard in the past. It would be a nice oasis where they could have privacy and plant a little English-style garden while leaving sufficient grass for Babette to do her business. It was these times that having an engineer in the family paid off big-time. Bob measured the front yard and drew up several different designs. They planned and schemed to select the best layout. Then Bob went to the City of Fairfield to be certain that no building codes were violated and a permit was not warranted. They spent hours at the hardware store to select the perfect building materials and came to a final decision. It was a fun family project.

Fortunately, they had a spacious front yard with which to plan. They could build a block wall in the front with footers placed deeply enough that Babette couldn't tunnel under the fence. They told themselves that not only would they enjoy the space, but it would also add to the value of the house. That was their story, and they were sticking to it.

The courtyard would encompass half the front yard. The present chain-link fence would be removed. Behind the willow tree, a block wall covered by beige stucco the same color as the house and topped by bricks would be built. They would put an unobtrusive, clear round window of Plexiglas in the front corner of the fence so it wouldn't seem claustrophobic and so Babette could still interact with her friends. A bubbling, ground-level fountain could be installed for ambience and to provide water for Babette if it got too hot. Two low planters topped with black wrought iron on either side of the yard were added to the plan to plant herbs and brilliantly colored flowers of all varieties: red bougainvilleas, white lilies, yellow daisies, and pink roses to match the ones growing in the front planter. Brick pavers like those topping the stucco wall would be used to fashion a deck area for potted plants, a small patio table with chairs, and a comfortable lounge chair to spread out on and read a good book. Even a front-yard barbecue could be installed to make eating in the front yard convenient. With the plans finished, it was time to get in a work crew to build it.

Kat started with the PennySaver to search for a contractor. There were always lots of gardeners advertising for work; most of them were licensed and bonded contractors—a condition upon which her engineer husband insisted. She began calling numbers from the front of the list and setting up appointments for free estimates. Over the next week, she scheduled five contractors to come to the house, review the plans, and give an estimate of their best price. Bob would make the final decision and award the job based on his research with the Better Business Bureau and the state contractors' licensing board.

The first contractor was scheduled at eight o'clock on Monday morning. He came at twelve o'clock. This was a red flag as far as Kat was concerned. It reflected badly on his work ethic and told a tale of his unreliability. The one thing that *everyone* has is an equal amount of is time. Some people may be brighter, some people may be richer, and some people may be more skilled, but everyone has the same amount of time. Kat saw time as a precious commodity that, without exception, one spent on those things most important. To be four hours late was disrespectful and made it apparent that this job was not a priority to that contractor. The gentleman left his estimate, which Kat filed immediately in the garbage.

The next contractor was a ragtag outfit, and though the PennySaver ad promised a contractor's license, Kat had her doubts. He showed up in a barely running black pickup truck with the words Pete's Gardening painted in white letters on the side. He spoke with Kat about the plans, asking the same questions several times, scrawled an impossibly low estimate on an In-N-Out napkin, and said good-bye. This estimate was likewise filed in the garbage can. In fact, of the many contractors interviewed by Kat, there were only two that seemed reputable. One gentleman named Grayson was knowledgeable and professional. He employed a five-man work crew, so he promised the job could be knocked out in a timely fashion.

The second contractor under consideration was less experienced and had just himself and one other employee. While he underbid Grayson, he would require twice the time to finish the project and couldn't start right away as he was booked with another job for the next two weeks.

Bob looked on the Better Business Bureau website and found no derogatory reports on either businessman and went to the Professional Contractors website to validate the contractors' licenses. All things being equal, Grayson had promised the quickest turnaround, probably in two weeks, and that his crew would start work immediately, so the deal was cinched.

When the crew came on Monday, Kat answered the door. Babette went berserk to find five men standing on the other side. Kat said hello to Grayson and introduced herself to the other four men, one of whom, Javier, leered nastily at Kat like he was drooling over an ice cream sundae. Javier had long, greasy black hair held back with a Raiders ball cap and a deeply olive complexion. His sharp nose had a bump in the midnasal spine that was likely the result of a fracture in the past. Tattoos covered his body and neck, and a tattooed teardrop adorned a corner of his left eye. Kat ignored his rudeness and spoke directly to Grayson, but she had a creepy feeling and could feel him continuing to gawk at her. Grayson explained that he would be leaving two of his men there to begin the demolition and outlined a plan for the project. He spent about fifteen minutes with a two-man crew on reviewing how to proceed then left.

There was a knock at the door an hour later. Kat and Babette answered the door; Javier was standing there with an impudent look on his face. Babette went insane, barking and hopping toward Javier with undisguised aggression. She growled, snarled, and actually had a line of hackles standing up the middle of her back. Kat was astonished. Hackles? Babette? She didn't even know she could do that. "Yes?" Kat asked.

Javier said, "Oh, *Mamasita*. Could I trouble you for a glass of water?"

He leaned into the doorway entirely too close, invading Kat's personal space. Kat reacted involuntarily with disgust, which actually seemed to please Javier. She had all she could do to corral Babette; she wanted to take a chunk out of Javier. Babette had never actually bit anyone in anger before. Twice she had nipped someone because it was an emergency and she could find no other way to communicate, but this was entirely different. She meant to attack this man in earnest.

Kat said, "Just a minute." She closed the door and picked up Babette in a death grip to restrain her while she got a sleeve of paper cups and returned. She opened the door, and Babette went back into full-attack mode.

Javier peered into the open door and said, "Senora, you have a beautiful home. Many pretty things." He leered at her as he said this with an oily look. Then he looked at Babette and said, "That's a mean dog you have there. Little dogs are often mean. I hope she never bites anyone. The dog-pound people, they don't like that." This was said pointedly and meant to be a threat to Babette.

"Here are some clean cups. Use the hose for water," Kat said dismissively and closed the door. But she was shaking, and Babette was practically having an out-of-body experience.

If Kat found Javier's demeanor around her objectionable, she was even more offended by his inappropriate attention to Greta. When he saw her, he would call her *Mija* and try to touch her in some way. "I'll get your nose!" Or he would try to tickle her. Often he would pick one of the pink roses growing in the front planter, strip the thorns off, and hand it ceremonially to Greta. Greta would always accept the rose from him but with an uncharacteristic deadpan expression on her face. Greta was known for her sunny disposition, but around Javier, she never cracked a smile. Also, normally a chatterbox, she refused to respond to him verbally. This frightened Kat because she believed children and animals to be the best judges of character, and both Babette and Greta had gone on record with their unfavorable assessment. He was a scumbag.

Should I make a federal case out of it? She wondered. *I can take care of myself,* she thought. *I don't have to go running to Bob or Grayson. I've made my point. Just let it go.*

She called Jeannine though and told her that the guy was a jerk. She asked her to drop by and pick her and Babette up to walk up to the kindergarten classes to pick up the kids. After Jeanine got there, the two women walked past Javier, ignoring him as his eyes insultingly devoured the two. Babette wanted nothing more than to tear this guy up. She could barely contain herself most of the way to school. Kat was appalled at Babette's hostile reaction to Javier causing her to be even more uncomfortable around him. *It's OK. I'm OK,* Kat tried to reassure herself. *After all, I'm a grown woman.*

The work on the front yard continued not at the lightning speed as Grayson originally promised but at a snail's pace. Babette was necessarily relegated to walks to relieve herself as the fence had now been demolished, but more importantly, she could not be trusted out in the front yard because of her intense dislike for Javier. Had she the chance, she would have cheerfully torn out his throat, and Javier felt the same way about Babette. Babette sat nervously at attention, stared at the doggy door, and alternately whined or growled for the majority of the time the work crew was in the front yard.

Javier had a million excuses to knock at the front door: Could he use the restroom? Could he get some ice for his drink? Could Kat put his lunch in the microwave to heat it up? Every interaction was rife with greasy innuendo. He had a way of delivering a compliment that made it necessary to take a shower. "Ah, Senora, you are a beautiful, sexy woman. I hope that husband of yours is treating you right."

What he didn't say was worse than what he did say. His body language and drooling were constantly suggestive. Kat put Babette in another room at first when Javier would knock to use the restroom because she feared Babette would attack the slimeball, giving him license to harm her. But once Babette was locked in the bedroom, Javier would stall, make unforgiveable comments, and leer. At least with Babette in the mix and making a ruckus, Kat could rush Javier back outside.

Kat dreaded getting up in the morning to face Javier's onslaught. She told herself that if she were going to have peace again that she would need to grow a spine and set Javier straight. So the next time he started telling her things like "You have the body of a dancer," she decided to take a stand. "I don't appreciate those types of comments. My husband would not like it, and I don't like it."

He continued to leer at her and grinned. He enjoyed eliciting a reaction from Kat. That infuriated her. This had gone on long enough. She said quietly through clenched teeth, "If you value your job, you'd better back off, goon."

Javier's face grew dark and menacing. "You think you're too good for me? You think you could only love a man like your husband? I am just as good as he is." He took a couple of steps toward her, and suddenly, she didn't feel so brave. Just then, Babette struggled to get loose and attacked Javier. She bit him on the right ankle, and he flicked his foot and kicked her in the side hard. She rolled over and sprung right back up, lunging for Javier.

Kat scooped Babette up. She was a bundle of fury. "You get out of this house, Javier, and off my property," Kat spoke evenly. He seemed to consider it. Kat reached for the phone, preparing to call 911 for help, but it was a bluff because had he wanted to jerk the phone out of her hand, then she and Babette would be unprepared to defend themselves. She changed her tactics and started screaming instead. He left slamming the front door as he went.

Kat stroked Babette's sides, searching for a broken rib or other injury. She was practically hysterical when she called Bob. He promised to come home, but it would take a frightening twenty minutes for him to reach her from work. Javier had not left. He was in the front yard, leaning on a rack, escalating and talking to the other worker angrily.

Fortunately, Grayson showed up before Bob made it home. Bob had called him from work to tell him there was a problem. Grayson stopped in the front yard and dismissed the two workers before knocking at the front door. They left with Javier, peeling rubber down the street.

Kat was crying when she let him in. Grayson said he was on another jobsite just around the corner when Bob called, and he came over to see what was going on. Kat explained that Javier had been hitting on her since they started the job and getting increasingly bolder. She told him that at first it seemed merely disrespectful but recently had taken on a predatory tone that made her uncomfortable. Kat refused to have Javier on the premises from then on, and that was nonnegotiable.

Bob walked in to Grayson trying to calm Kat, reassuring her that Javier would not be working on this project any longer. Later, Kat discovered that Grayson fired Javier. Javier had been a cousin twice removed, and Grayson gave Javier a job as a favor to a family member. It was a trial run, and Grayson was disappointed with the quality of Javier's work, to say the least, but this was the final straw to find out that Javier had been tormenting Kat.

Grayson worked the job after that. He brought in several workers, making rapid progress. Once or twice Kat thought she saw Javier drive by the house but told herself it was all in her head. The truth was she just didn't feel safe.

Once the courtyard was finished, the couple had a yard-warming party. It was really just an excuse to have a block party for friends to come together. Many people brought plants as gifts for the new garden, offering advice on where they might look best. It was a BYOM (bring your own meat) party, so people came with steaks or hot dogs or hamburgers or chicken—even soy burgers, which were brought by a vegan family. Bob had the barbecue fired up to cook up whatever anybody wanted. There was a picnic table set up along the side laden with covered dishes, potato salad, watermelon, and homemade cakes.

The front yard was populated with children laughing and playing and dogs frolicking. Lots of neighborhood dogs came. Wilber was there to represent basset hounds everywhere with his ears brushing on the ground as he walked.

Hector arrived strolling grandly into the yard with a strut that would have made Fonzie from *Happy Days* jealous. Babette spotted him immediately and scurried toward him like the Energizer Bunny on caffeine. She played coy by wiggling seductively, rolling on her back to show him her pretty belly and generally just making a darn fool of herself. You could almost hear the song by Salt-n-Pepa playing in the background. "Whatta man, Whatta man, whatta man, whatta man, whatta mighty good man." Hector had his image to consider, so he merely regarded her with aloofness but nudged her with his nose as a consolation, which seemed to satisfy her. He made the rounds, greeting everyone and helping himself to a hot dog if he felt like it. Who could stop him? At 180 pounds, Hector called the shots within limits. He sauntered up to Dale, who was sitting in a comfy, double-wide, red-flowered patio chair. Dale was a friend who was also a neighbor from the next block over and a cat lover, of all things. Hector sniffed him with disdain. He rose up on his back paws, placing one front paw firmly on either of Dale's shoulders pinning him in place. Then he proceeded to make his position on cat lovers evident. It's not unknown for a dog to hump someone's leg. A dog is, after all, a dog, and this type of behavior more often is a matter of dominance than what you might think it is. While nobody likes it, one usually just brushes the dog off good-naturedly. But this was something fearsome. As Hector and Dale almost made puppies, Dale shrieked a high-pitched squeal like a little girl, screaming, "Get him off of me! Get him off of me!" It wasn't that Hector's owner didn't want to help; it was just that he couldn't stop laughing long enough to lend assistance. After Dale was rescued, he found it hard to get past the whole thing and went home in a snit. Hector, though, stayed at the party, looking immensely pleased with himself.

The men tended to gravitate to one side to discuss politics and sports while the women swapped recipes and spoke at length about their families on the other. Everyone pitched in to help with the children, orchestrating spats and kissing minor boo-boos. It felt like a big extended family.

After eating, someone brought out a soft big red ball and challenged everyone to a game of no-holds-barred dodge ball. A couple of the adults scoffed, maybe considering themselves too sophisticated to play a child's game like dodge ball, but acquiesced in the end, and the teams were divvied up by team captains Jeannine and Kat. Only one rule applied: husbands and wives had to be on opposite teams.

The game took on new strategy with husbands and wives pitted against each other. There was a lot of cheating, like when Jeanine jumped on Art's back and covered his eyes with her hands so he couldn't see to throw the ball. He ran around blindly with her perched on his back and lobbed the ball like she wasn't there.

Alia had a foolproof strategy. She flashed her husband at the opportune time, causing him to lose concentration and toss the ball on the roof. One of the guys was able to dodge the ball or skillfully throw it with a cold beer clutched in one hand without spilling a drop at the immense admiration of the other men. Hector kept absconding with the ball, but if he were coaxed with a wiener, he would bring it back on command. The children were incorporated into the game and afforded do-overs with adults purposely taking a hit to sacrifice themselves making certain a good time was had by everyone.

Kat was having a great time until she looked up to get a bead on Greta. She searched the yard and found her sitting in the corner next to the Plexiglas window that had been built into the fence overlooking the street. There she sat. In her hand was a single pink rose. Kat's blood ran cold in her veins when she saw that rose. When Kat checked the rose, she found that the thorns had been stripped away.

Javier had obviously been there but went unnoticed because of the confusion. That creep had interacted with her little girl. It felt like a threat—like "See? I could have taken her if I had wanted." Kat was beside herself. She wanted to call the police and get a restraining order. Bob reasoned that she didn't have much in the way of evidence. A rose would not impress a judge sufficiently to warrant a restraining order. He tried to reassure her that maybe Greta had picked the rose herself, ignoring the fact that the thorns had been stripped away. Kat was not placated.

Kat spied Javier around the neighborhood several times. One time, she was positive he drove slowly past the house in an old beat-up Toyota, giving Kat the heebie-jeebies. Once he sat in his car at the end of the street as Jeanine and Kat walked by to pick up the kids. She recognized his familiar leer, but now there was an undercurrent of almost tangible anger. Jeanine and Kat made a valiant effort to ignore Javier, but the pink rose at the party and the sightings around the neighborhood were taking their toll on her. She looked both ways before walking outside and peeked around every corner. She began seeing him around the neighborhood whether he was there or not. She was a nervous wreck.

Bob spent a lot of time talking Kat down. "He's a bully, Kat. He's mad because he lost his job and because you didn't knuckle under him when he tried to intimidate you," he conjoled. What Bob didn't know was that Javier had won on some level. Kat was genuinely scared enough that it was impacting her life. She could feel no peace.

Friday night came around, traditionally a joyous occasion for the little family. Friday night was family night and date night. After a long week of working and nursing classes and, well, just life, Friday nights were reserved as sacred and spent just by the four of them as a family.

That night, they went out to their favorite Italian restaurant for dinner, Spaghetti Freddie's. There was an outside seating area with hanging plastic grapes and twinkling lights, so Babette was welcome to come along. Luigi, the owner of the restaurant, was a Renaissance man who greeted customers with a warm hug and a kiss planted on both cheeks. Babette and he were buds, and when he came to greet them, he always snuck her some treat: a piece of prosciutto or a meatball. There was a man after Babette's own heart. Yes, a meatball yet.

Dinner was scrumptious. They started with antipasto: salami, cheeses, olives, and Bibb lettuce with vinegar and olive oil dressing. Bob ordered the spaghetti carbonara as the main course, his personal favorite Italian dish from the good old days when he and Kat had first met in Italy. Kat loved the eggplant parmesan, the finest eggplant parmesan stateside anywhere. Greta had rigatoni, tomatoey goodness with yummy pasta that Greta always ordered. Babette had bites of everything and gave it all her personal approval.

It was nine o'clock by the time they got home. Bob carried a sleeping Greta in from the car. It was bedtime for Greta and quiet alone time for the adults. Kat and Bob lay Greta down for the night, holding hands and watching her sleep for the miracle she was.

Date night was anticipated all week long. It put the day-to-day trials and crises in perspective as they reflected on the true importance of their marriage. Things might go wrong at work or Greta might be fighting off a cold, but if they could just make it to Friday night, Kat could crawl up in Bob's arms, and everything would make sense. They watched an old movie together—a charming Jimmy Stewart masterpiece called *Harvey* that was about a six-foot pooka rabbit. Then they turned in for the night with garlic from Spaghetti Freddie's still rich in their mouths.

The digital alarm clock read 3:00 AM when Kat was awakened by Babette's frantic barking. It was emanating from Greta's bedroom. There were times when Midnight kitty raided the front yard or some other animal thoughtlessly ventured onto the property that Babette sounded the alarm, but from the tone of her barking, this was not a drill. Chills ran up Kat's spine as she elbowed a sleepy Bob and screamed, "Get up, get up!" She didn't wait for Bob but ran into the hallway and around the corner to Greta's bedroom.

She sped into Greta's room. As her eyes adjusted to the light, she saw a man's shadow silhouetted against the window. There was no question in her mind. It was Javier, and he held Greta in his arms. Kat could hear Babette snarling as she savaged Javier's ankles. He kicked her against the wall repeatedly, but she snapped right back, undaunted. Kat's eyes went to Javier's face; he was triumphantly smiling, his face one of pure rage. He seemed to have gone over the edge of sanity and down the other side. Kat was more scared than she had ever been in her life.

"Put her down, Javier," Kat ordered. She was struggling not to surrender to all-out panic.

Javier grinned with malice and said, "Ah, my love, I have come back. I have the upper hand. How do you like me now?"

"Look, Javier, whatever you want, we can work this out. I'll leave my husband. I was just playing hard to get. I've always had a thing for you." Kat forced a strained smile and tried to look alluring.

Javier merely laughed. "No, I don't think that it's possible for you to love me. You're spoiled and ungrateful. But Greta, I could teach her to be humble. I could teach her obedience with the proper discipline. And it would be just the punishment you deserve for thinking you are too good for me."

Kat tried to keep a cool head and reason with Javier. "Please, honey. You know I love you. Put Greta down on the bed, and I'll show you. We belong together."

Javier purposely squeezed Greta, making her squeal in pain. "Get out of my way, Kat. Or I'll kill her. I mean it." He began walking toward the door.

All attempts to maintain any composure were gone. Kat was screaming and moving toward Javier, but for every forward step she took, he hurt Greta, causing Kat to back up. She was pleading, crying. It was his game. If she advanced on Javier, he caused Greta pain, and there was no telling how far he might have gone to hurt her and punish Kat. She believed he meant to kill Greta; she could read it in his eyes

Just as Javier reached the doorway, Babette jumped from the top of the clothes hamper and aimed directly for Javier's face. She clamped on to Javier's right cheek and right eye with the strength of a pit bull and refused to let go. Now it was his turn to feel what it was like to have one's hands tied with no recourse. The harder he tugged with one hand to dislodge Babette, the more damage he caused to his face and eye because she relentlessly locked her jaw. With Javier distracted by Babette, Kat lunged, her knee targeting Javier's groin, landing hard, causing him to drop Greta and slink to the floor. Babette was still connected to his face. Kat managed to deliver one more satisfying, well-placed kick to his left kidney area then grabbed Greta and fled the room.

Javier knew Kat was escaping. He drew a fist, slamming it into the little dog. She sagged limply and released her hold. He pulled her from his face and slammed her into the wall, where she slid to the floor and lay still.

Kat ran from Greta's room toward the bathroom—the only room with a lock, such as it was. As she passed the master bedroom, she nearly crashed into Bob, fully awake now and charging down the hall after Javier. She prayed that Bob could hold his own against the thug, knowing that Bob's experience as a gangster was maybe one fight over a barstool in a barroom when he was young.

Kat slammed the bathroom door and locked it. She threw towels in the tub and laid a hysterical Greta on top. If Javier bested Bob, she knew that bathroom lock would not turn Javier for long. Kat stood to open the window and caught a glimpse of her face in the medicine-cabinet mirror, the face of a woman who was ready to kill without a qualm. She opened the bathroom window above the tub and screamed for help repeatedly—as loudly as if her family's life depended on it because it very likely did.

In the other part of the house, Bob burst through Greta's bedroom door to see Javier bleeding and still disoriented from pain. Bob used this moment's advantage to deliver a blow to Javier's face. Javier fell backward and knocked his head against the dresser with a thunk! Javier was dazed but still swung blindly upward with his right fist, catching Bob under the jaw and driving him off. Blood spurted from both men, but neither slowed in their assault. This was what Javier wanted. He wanted to take it out on Bob because Bob led a life Javier would never lead. Maybe it was a simple life according to some standards but was decent and unobtainable to Javier. Bob had a wife who loved him, a modest little house, a professional career, and a healthy daughter, and he was respected as a member of his community. Maybe in the grand scheme of things, these were the genuinely important things in life. Javier was driven by jealousy and a lifetime of failure, but the stakes were high for Bob. He fought for the safety of his family. Kat could hear the dull thumps of fists as the two men battled. It seemed interminable.

Kat heard someone ring the doorbell and pound at the door. "Kat, Bob, open up."

Kat recognized Art's voice and screamed "Help!" from the bathroom.

Art pounded harder at the front door then said, "Last chance, guys. Then I break the window." The glass from the sidelight next to the door tinkled as Art broke out the window to unlock the door. She could hear the door open and footsteps running through the living room. Kat knew that Art kept his police-issue gun at his house. She prayed he had thought to bring it with him. She got her answer about the gun as two loud bangs echoed through the house. Then she heard only silence.

Kat cowered in the tub, holding Greta. Greta had stopped crying and instead sat listlessly in Kat's arms, repeating, "Waa-Waa tried to get me," using a term she had not used since she was a toddler. It was disconcerting. Kat was plenty worried about the stoic expression on Greta's little face. Greta was not making eye contact and wouldn't respond to questions. She wanted to reassure her, but she had no clear idea of what they still had to face, so she couldn't bear to lie to her.

There was a soft knocking at the door. "Come on out, Kat. Come on now. Is Greta OK? Come on, honey. It's Jeanine."

No response. Kat was terrified of what she might find. Would she find her husband dead? Was Jeanine being coerced by Javier to encourage Kat to vacate the bathroom? Who took the bullets?

The bathroom door buckled and hit the wall as it was forced open. Kat was trembling with hate as she readied herself to do battle to protect Greta. She set her jaw, picked up a magazine rack lying beside the toilet, and said out loud, "Oh yeah, it's on." She felt the adrenaline coursing through her veins as her heart hammered. She turned her head toward the open bathroom door, feeling like this was a scene in a movie. In her present state, she nearly didn't register the fact that standing there was not Javier but a bloodied Bob. Her husband was alive. She couldn't be sure how badly hurt he was. His face was a bloody pulp, and it looked like his jaw was broken, but regardless, the family had survived. Bob walked slowly forward and tried to pull Greta from the tub, but Kat dropped the towel rack and stooped grasping Greta protectively. He put both arms around Kat and tried to stand her up, but she adamantly refused to leave the tub. He decided to simply sit quietly beside her; reassuring them both that everything was going to be fine. Jeanine came into the bathroom and perched on the side of the tub, trying to coax Kat out. That's when the police arrived.

There was a lot of commotion, but Kat was in no condition to speculate on what was happening. She could count three policemen and hear additional sirens approaching the house. The static from the policemen's radios pierced the din. She could make out a 911 call for an ambulance that filled her with fear. Who? Was it Art? Had he been hurt badly enough to need an ambulance? Where was Javier?

No sooner had the ambulance arrived than it left again. Kat could hear more static from the radios, and this time, the police requested a medical examiner. Someone had died.

Kat looked into Bob's face and asked, "Is Art OK? Did Javier get away? Where's Babette?"

Bob pointed to Greta and mouthed silently, "Not in front of Greta."

Out loud, he said, "Art is fine. The police have Javier. Everything is OK. You and Greta can come out of the tub. You're safe now."

Gradually, Kat allowed Bob to take Greta from her. Greta willingly crawled into her daddy's arms and wrapped her arms around his neck. She knew a safe haven when she saw one. "The Waa-Waa, Daddy," she mumbled.

Bob offered his hand to Kat to help her stand up. She had no idea how long she had crouched in the tub, but it must have been a long, long time because her legs barely held her as she stood. The three walked into the master bedroom and sat huddled together on the bed wrapped in a blanket.

Slowly Kat began to take inventory of the people she loved. Greta was still pale and still babbling about the Waa-Waa, which worried Kat, but she seemed to be physically sound. Bob's face and right hand were bleeding, and she was certain now that his jaw was broken, but he seemed to be healthy otherwise. Kat could hear the police talking to Art, so he must have been OK. Kat vaguely remembered seeing Jeanine uninjured in the bathroom. She felt a sinking feeling in her gut as she wondered out loud, "Where's Babette?"

As if Bob read her mind, he said, "Last time I saw Babette, she was in Greta's room," he said noncommittally.

The police appeared in the master-bedroom doorway with questions. Bob asked that they interview one parent at a time so the other parent could shield and comfort Greta. She had had enough for one night; the police agreed and asked to speak to Kat first. Before Kat would answer any question of theirs, she had a few of her own. "Where's Javier?" she asked.

The police gave their account of what occurred. Jeanine had been keeping Art apprised of the situation with Javier. Art had a policeman's sixth sense for trouble, probably what kept him alive. They had heard Kat calling from the bathroom because their bedroom window was on the same side as Kat's bathroom window. Art's sixth sense kicked in. The police received a 911 call from Art and Jeanine before the couple left their house to go to Bob and Kat's front door. Art broke the window, unlocked the door, and found Bob and Javier in Greta's bedroom with Bob taking a pretty good beating. Art was armed with his police-issue Colt. He took a bead on Javier. "Lay down on the floor," he ordered. Javier turned to face Art, cussing and threatening him. Diverting Javier's attention gave Bob the opportunity to get up and look for his wife and child. According to the police, after Bob left the room, Javier charged Art who shot him twice: once in the left shoulder and a second fatal shot to the chest.

Kat endured the questioning numbly for what seemed like hours and then held Greta while Bob was interrogated. The process probably was less of a headache than it might have been because of Art's status as a Fairfield police officer and his knowledge of the situation. As soon as Bob could shoulder Greta's care, Kat went to Greta's room, peering inside.

There was Babette lying still on the floor between the clothes hamper and the wall. Kat could see no blood. She knelt beside the small dog, calling her name softly. "Hey, Babette. You did it. You saved your kid."

Babette did not move. Kat lay down beside her and gently stroked her fur. "Babette, come on, Babette." She lay face-to-face with her dear friend. "Are you OK?"

Babette opened one eye, giving Kat hope. Kat petted her dear friend's face, thinking of Babette when she was a tiny, furry ball of terror playing fetch and charming children. She thought about all the lives Babette had touched and maybe even saved: Esmeralda, Margaret, Greta's beloved grandmother, and in fact, Kat and Greta owed Babette their lives from the time during the difficult pregnancy. She thought of Bob's near-drowning episode and the empty lifetime she was spared as a result of Babette's courage. She celebrated Babette's unconditional love and selfless loyalty. In her heart, she knew it had been an honor to be Babette's owner. When one considered the astonishing capabilities, it seemed evident that Babette was special with some pretty remarkable abilities, but then, any dog owner must likely feel that way about their pet.

"Babette, Babette." Tears streamed down Kat's face as she scratched Babette's ears, calling to her. She stroked Babette's neck, and just then, the little dog's pink tongue appeared briefly and licked Kat's hand. Then Kat watched the light flicker from her Babette's eyes, and she was gone.